CAPE CORRAL KEEPER

SALTWATER COWBOYS, BOOK 3

CHRISTY BARRITT

River Heights

CHAPTER ONE

TEARS PRESSED at Gracie Loveland's eyes.

She gripped the side of the boat as white caps crashed around her.

It wasn't even stormy, but a strong breeze churned up the open expanse of water surrounding her. A briny scent rose with the turbulence as the skiff rocked back and forth.

Gathering herself, she stumbled toward the back of the boat and tried the motor again. It was no use.

The engine was dead.

Gracie's head spun as she considered her options, trying to remain calm.

Panicking will get you nowhere. That's what her dad had always taught her.

Yet she felt powerless against the lure of the emotion—especially since panic seemed like her only option right now.

She was on a boat. In the middle of who-knows-where. With tempestuous waters.

In a wedding dress.

Think, Gracie. Think!

She squeezed her eyes shut, forcing herself to focus. There had to be a solution here.

When she opened her eyes again, she spotted trees in the distance across the stretch of water—probably a hundred feet away.

Gracie could make it there. Maybe even swim if she had to.

But what would she do when she reached the shore?

She wasn't sure.

She just knew she had to get off this boat. Going out in these conditions had been a terrible idea. No doubt there was a small craft advisory.

But she hadn't had time to think—only to act.

Her future had depended on it.

Gracie pressed her eyes shut again, trying to gain her balance.

Everything around her continued to spin. Could

the stress she'd been under for the past month really make her this dizzy?

As another wave of lightheadedness seized her, she gripped the moisture-splattered edge of the skiff, her French-tipped nails digging into the fiberglass structure.

Squeezing her eyes shut again, Gracie prayed everything would right itself in her world.

In more ways than one.

But that wasn't possible.

Maybe it wouldn't ever be a possibility.

A cry caught in her throat at the thought.

Just as it seemed the spinning around her might end, another wave rocked the boat, nearly sending her sideways.

Everything twirled around her again.

Maybe all the tears she'd cried had left her dehydrated. Maybe the stress of having someone she'd trusted betray her had battered her heart until only emptiness resounded. Maybe her life as a whole was such a sore disappointment that her mind was rebelling.

Another wave hit the boat, jostling it so hard the craft nearly tipped.

As the vessel lurched, Gracie felt herself tumbling.

Over the edge of the boat.

Into the choppy water surrounding her.

She tried to push herself back to the surface. But her wedding dress entombed her. She couldn't tell which way was up.

The weight of the gown pulled her down. The folds of her exquisite fabric promised to be the most beautiful murder weapon ever.

Gracie's lungs screamed for air as she fought her dress, trying to free her arms.

It was no use.

Exhaustion already began to weaken her muscles.

She needed to breathe!

She needed help!

But there was no one around to assist her.

Gracie knew she wouldn't get out of this alone.

Yet that was exactly what she was.

Alone.

Now and forever.

A cry caught in her throat as the water overwhelmed her.

DILLON MCGRATH GRIPPED his phone as he rode horseback near the edge of the forest, acting as temporary patrol for Cape Corral. His normal role was fire chief, but everyone chipped in here on the island when needed. They were one man down right now since Levi Sutherland was on his honeymoon.

Dillon didn't mind filling in. The late autumn day had a brisk wind that churned up the water, despite the glaring sun overhead. The wild horses seemed to be enjoying the change in temperature. He'd already spotted ten of the island's four hundred or so original inhabitants.

It was the perfect day to be outside with his horse, Blaze.

"While you're out by Wash Woods, keep your eyes open for any sign of the stolen skiff," Grant Matthews, one of Dillon's colleagues, said over the phone line. "It was taken from the harbor across the water and reported missing a few hours ago. The marine police are caught up in a drug bust farther south, but authorities think the boat is headed this way."

"Will do."

"One more thing while I have you on the line," Grant continued. "The guys and I are trying to brainstorm some ideas to raise awareness about our wild horses on the island. The more people who care about them, the more funds we can raise. The more funds we raise, the more easily we can provide for the horses' care and give them a safe environment."

"Makes sense."

"Plus, I'm afraid the Fergusons are going to file a lawsuit over these land acquisitions they've made and all the razzle-dazzle around them."

The Fergusons were a wealthy family who'd moved to the island a decade ago. They had been buying up property so they could build a resort. But the traffic would seriously endanger the wild horse population—not to mention the island didn't have the infrastructure for something like that.

"You think it will go that far?" Dillon asked.

"Thomas Ferguson is throwing everything at this," Grant said. "An article just came out in *Carolina Coast Monthly* about their plans to make this area a tourist attraction. It was very convincing, and I worry if too many people get behind this, we're going to lose."

Dillon didn't like the sound of that.

"I'll see if I can come up with any ideas," Dillon said.

"Put your thinking cap on," Grant said. "We'll chat again when Levi gets back."

"Sounds good. Later." Dillon shoved his phone back in his pocket and nudged Blaze. The horse began strolling near the edge of the Currituck Sound.

As much as Dillon liked fighting fires and taking rescue calls, there was something soothing about patrolling the island alone. He'd never been one to mind solitude. Most of the people who moved to Cape Corral would say the same. No one came to this stretch of sand for the nightlife or the excitement of an action-packed schedule—because those things didn't exist here.

People came for the windswept beaches, for the smell of the ocean, and for the tranquility of watching the wild horses that roamed these shores.

It was why Dillon had come here four years ago. He'd visited once with a friend when they'd been stationed in Norfolk. Dillon had instantly fallen in love with the area. After Dillon's term of service with the military ended, and while nursing a broken heart, he'd applied on the island to be a firefighter. Two years ago, he'd become chief.

As his horse ambled along, Dillon glanced at the water bordering the west side of the island. It was different than the Atlantic. Unlike the ocean, there were no huge waves or sudden drop-offs.

The Currituck was generally peaceful, a nursery for marine life like horseshoe crabs, oysters, and bull sharks. Shallow water stretched for almost a half mile before dropping deeper into the channel, making it a waterman's paradise. Today, however, whitecaps dotted the normally placid surface.

Dillon tugged the reins in his hands as he spotted something on the horizon. "Whoa, boy."

A skiff jostled in the water, not terribly far away.

Was this the boat Grant had mentioned?

Dillon squinted, trying to see what the person aboard was doing.

But it was hard to make out many details from his vantage point. Best he could tell, there was one person on the vessel. Possibly a woman.

Was she wearing . . . white?

It almost looked like she wore a dress.

A . . . wedding dress?

In Dillon's years on the island, he'd seen stranger things, he supposed. People dressed in inflatable T-Rex costumes running a race by the ocean. Miles of potatoes washed up from a shipwreck. College kids trying to recreate a scene from *Aquaman*.

But something about the woman's body

language, even from this far distance, put Dillon on edge.

The woman leaned over the boat, almost as if trying to hang on.

The next instant, she tumbled headfirst into the water.

CHAPTER TWO

AS GRACIE BEGAN to lose consciousness, a second wind revitalized her. Survival instinct kicked in, and her senses snapped with alertness.

Her wedding dress continued to rise up. To surround her.

To *trap* her.

Just like her almost-marriage had.

Gracie reached for the surface, trying to claw her way to air. Her lungs burned, desperate for oxygen. But tulle from the dress shackled her arms.

It was no use.

Her dress cloaked her until everything blurred together.

Of all the ways Gracie had thought she might die this wasn't one of them.

Tears wanted to escape from her eyes. Maybe they *did* escape. Maybe they blended with her watery grave.

How had her life come to this moment?

Gracie had been praying for the last month that she'd find a way to make things right.

But no answers had come.

There wasn't a way to fix the mess she'd found herself in.

Deep inside, she knew that.

She should have accepted the fact when Constantine proposed.

Now she'd moved from one awful situation into another one.

CONCERN JOLTED through Dillon as he headed in the woman's direction. Why hadn't she surfaced yet?

He nudged Blaze as they galloped through the still-shallow water. "Faster, boy. Faster!"

Something was definitely wrong.

As the Currituck rose higher around his legs, Dillon jerked the reins, signaling his stallion to stop. This was as far as the horse could go.

Instead, Dillon dove into the water and propelled himself through the brackish liquid toward the woman. He came up for air and tried to locate her.

She'd gone over this side of the boat.

But where was she now?

A puff of white appeared ahead. The sight almost reminded him of a . . . jellyfish.

This was no jellyfish.

Dillon knew that.

It was the woman's dress.

The clothing was so heavy she must have become entangled in it.

Concern ricocheted through Dillon.

He kicked his legs, the motion thrusting him through the water until he reached her. Dillon dove deeper, grabbed the woman around her waist, and shot to the surface. Somehow, he managed to leverage the woman on his shoulder.

As he broke through the water, he noticed her body was nearly limp. Carefully, Dillon grabbed the edge of the small boat that jostled in the rough water.

He had to figure out a way to get her inside.

Treading water, Dillon boosted the woman higher until her body draped over the side of the boat. He pulled himself up and over the side then lifted her the rest of the way in.

Moving quickly, Dillon grabbed layer upon layer of silky, white material and pulled them down until he found the woman's face.

Her *lifeless* face.

He leaned close to her mouth, trying to feel her breath.

Just as he did, she sprang to life. She coughed then catapulted herself into an upright position and drew in a long breath of air.

Her eyes widened with panic as she stared straight ahead, the whites appearing around her pupils.

As she coughed again, she broke from her spell and leaned against the side of the boat.

Something about her gaze almost made Dillon think she was shocked that she'd survived.

Had this woman fallen into the water on purpose?

That didn't matter right now. What mattered was that the woman wearing a drenched wedding gown in the middle of the Currituck Sound had survived. She might as well have had a ball and chain around her ankle.

She'd barely defeated her faceoff with death.

As Dillon leaned toward her, she screamed, "I know who you are, and I'm not going back! Only over my dead body."

CHAPTER THREE

GRACIE STARED at the man in front of her, panic claiming her every thought.

Where had he come from? What was he doing here? How had he found her?

The truth washed over her.

Her ex-fiancé had sent him, hadn't he?

Terror surged through her at the realization.

Strength Gracie didn't know she had erupted from her like a volcano. Her God-given instinct for survival surged to life.

"Get away from me!" Using both hands, she shoved the man away.

But the man didn't budge.

He was far too big. Too strong. Too muscular.

Gracie's moment of bravado turned into fear as she realized the gravity of the situation.

She couldn't defeat this man.

She was no match for his strength or size.

How was Gracie going to get out of this situation? Was this man trying to save her only for the purpose of bringing her back to that horrible family?

Because she wasn't going to go.

Gracie would fight with her life to make sure she was never entwined with Constantine's family again.

Her family's legacy depended on it.

Gracie stared at the man—a hulking man with muscles that put a commando to shame. Constantine's family certainly hadn't skimped on hiring the best to track her down. She shouldn't be surprised.

"I'm not going with you!" she repeated, her voice just below a growl.

Gracie raised her hands again, prepared to fight. She was going to make it as difficult as possible for this man to hurt her. She owed it to her parents to give this everything she had.

But before she could make another move, the man grabbed her wrists and anchored them in place. She fought to get out of his grasp, but there was no use. He easily overpowered her.

With that one move, she'd been rendered frozen, unable to escape.

"Calm down," the man murmured, his eyes latching onto hers. "It's going to be okay."

Something about his voice sounded reassuring.

Not threatening.

Not imposing.

Gracie took a deep breath and tried to think more clearly. Had she misjudged the situation? What if this man wasn't one of the bad guys?

"Who are you?" she demanded before a coughing attack took over. She mentally grumbled against the reaction. How could she sound tough while hacking up a lung?

But she couldn't let that stop her.

Gracie couldn't risk putting her guard down. Doing so might cost her life. Not physically. But her time would no longer be her own. She'd practically be a slave to the DiMarzio clan.

If that happened, she might as well be dead.

If her life wasn't hers to live, then why did anything matter?

It didn't.

"I'm Fire Chief Dillon McGrath from the Cape Corral Fire Department," the man explained, his brown eyes burning into hers. "I saw you fall over-board and came out to help."

A firefighter?

The man didn't look like any firefighter Gracie had ever seen. Black T-shirt, tight-fitting jeans, finely sculpted muscles . . .

Then again, what had she been expecting? A firetruck in the distance? Full gear in the middle of the water? A Dalmatian trailing behind him?

Still startled and ready to dart, Gracie glanced around. She needed to take in her surroundings. Think ahead. Figure out her next step.

Her gaze stopped at something in the distance.

Was that . . . a horse standing in the water?

Just as the thought raced through her mind, the man leaned over the side of the boat and plucked something from the water.

Was that a . . . cowboy hat?

Was Gracie missing something? She was in North Carolina, right? So why did she feel like she'd stepped into some East Coast island version of Texas?

"You're right offshore of Cape Corral," the man explained. "In case you don't know, the island is a wild horse sanctuary."

She blinked in confusion. "And you're a cowboy?"

The man set his wet hat on his head and pushed it back, a slight smile tugging at his lips. "Something like that."

Gracie opened her mouth, trying to find the words to respond. But she didn't even know what to say. Maybe she'd hit her head when she'd fallen overboard. Or maybe she was delirious right now.

The man examined her with his gaze. "Are you injured?"

She quickly did a self-evaluation, but nothing hurt—except maybe her pride. "I don't think so. I just lost my balance when a wave hit. My head was spinning, and the next thing I knew . . ."

His gaze narrowed with thought. "Do you ever get seasick?"

As the man asked the question, realization washed over Gracie. Why hadn't she realized that earlier? But her symptoms fit to a T.

"You know what?" she blurted. "That's probably it. I feel so foolish . . ."

But better to be foolish and alive than uninformed and dead.

That wasn't a forgone conclusion yet.

She was still far from being safe.

DILLON DIDN'T KNOW what was going on with this woman, but something had her frazzled.

More than frazzled.

She was frightened.

And wearing a wedding dress.

On a stolen boat.

In the middle of the sound.

Alone.

So many questions swirled in his head.

"I should take you back to the island and have the doctor check you, just to be safe," Dillon told her.

The woman's eyes widened, and she scooted back in the boat like a fawn scampering from danger.

"No, I'm fine," she rushed. "I don't need a doctor —or even want one, for that matter."

Dillon narrowed his eyes, her reaction taking him by surprise. "You don't look fine. We need to make sure you didn't hit your head or sustain any other injuries."

"I understand. But I need to get somewhere . . ." The woman glanced behind her and frowned, almost as if she expected to see someone there. "Time is . . . tight."

Where did she think she was going?

The perplexity of this woman continued to astound Dillon.

Finally, she turned back toward him, decision in her gaze. "Thank you for your help, but I'll be on my way now."

Dillon shook his head. "I am afraid that's not possible."

Her eyes widened even more. "What do you mean? I don't owe you anything. I said thank you. I don't mean to be rude, but I have a schedule to keep."

Dillon fought a smile. A schedule to keep? A woman in a wedding dress and on a boat in the middle of the Currituck Sound with a schedule to keep?

Was she headed to Cape Corral to get married? Because most women Dillon encountered wouldn't want to look waterlogged at their weddings.

The woman might be beautiful, but she was a sopping wet mess right now, complete with mascara running down her cheeks, stringy blonde hair, and a filthy, ripped dress.

"I'm sure you do have a schedule to keep." Dillon

tried to keep the amusement out of his voice. "But I'm going to need to bring you down to the station."

She sucked in a breath as she stared at him, eyes as wide as clams in a steamer. "Down to the station? It's not a crime to fall overboard."

"No, but it *is* a crime to steal a boat."

The woman opened her mouth as if to argue, but then quickly shut it again. She went through the same process again and again as if running through excuses but changing her mind when she realized none of them were valid.

Finally, with an almost feeble tone, she said, "I was going to return the boat."

Dillon raised an eyebrow.

He wasn't sure how the woman had intended on doing that.

But he looked forward to hearing her story.

Right after he arrested her for theft.

CHAPTER FOUR

GRACIE FELT the tension rising in her as the cowboy somehow managed to start the engine and they puttered toward the sandy shore in the distance.

As he did, he clucked his tongue, and his horse began to follow in the water beside them.

Again, that sense that she'd been sucked away by a tornado and placed in a whole new world filled her. Unlike Dorothy in Oz, Gracie couldn't cling to the mantra that there was no place like home.

Home was the last place she wanted to be.

When Gracie had taken this boat, she'd thought she was headed out into the Atlantic.

She wasn't sure what she'd been thinking.

She *hadn't* been thinking.

She'd just been desperate to get away.

A boat seemed faster than running, and the ocean seemed like the perfect place to hide.

In her mind, she'd idle down the coast until she eventually reached Florida.

Now that Gracie thought it through a little bit more, she realized she probably wouldn't have enough gas in the boat to make that happen.

But at the time, it hadn't mattered. All Gracie had wanted was to get away.

Far away.

She figured the rest of the details would fall in place.

At once, clarity hit her, and she realized that the boat trip would have been a terrible idea.

But so was this.

This man—Fire Chief Dillon McGrath—was going to charge her with stealing this boat. Gracie was going to spend what was supposed to be her wedding night in jail, wasn't she?

At once, an image of her in this designer wedding dress, still wet and pungent from the brackish water, sitting in a dingy cell filled her mind. At the thought of it, Gracie could almost feel the moisture settle into her lungs, and she coughed.

She was going from one prison to another.

A cry caught in her throat.

If this man knew Gracie had stolen this boat, who else knew?

Did Constantine?

Quickly, Gracie jerked her head to look behind her.

No other boats were in sight.

She released the air from her lungs in a temporary moment of relief.

She would get through this. As long as this firefighter cowboy didn't try to call any of her relatives, she should be fine.

Except she had no money to post bail.

No clothes.

No cell phone.

She had nothing.

Despair tried to bite even deeper.

How was she supposed to fight these charges with no possessions and no one on her side?

Gracie thought she'd reached the end of her rope back in that church before the wedding ceremony was supposed to start. But now it was clear that the pit she had fallen into was endless. She'd been cascading into darkness for a long time.

She was grateful that the man who'd commandeered the boat said nothing. Asked no questions.

Because Gracie wasn't in the mood to talk.

Finally, they reached a dock. Dillon seemed to know what he was doing as he puttered closer to the wooden structure and then tied a rope around one of the posts there. He killed the engine and stepped onto the wooden planks before reaching for her hand.

Gracie hesitated for just a moment. She wished she didn't need his assistance.

But this wedding dress probably weighed forty pounds soaking wet. There was no way she'd manage to get out of this boat on her own—not without falling on her face.

She hiked the skirt up as much as she could while remaining modest and then took his hand.

The strength the man used to pull her up shouldn't have surprised her. Gracie had seen his thick muscles.

But the motion had seemed effortless on his part.

Her part was a different story. Gracie nearly tumbled into the man's chest. Once both feet were firmly planted on the dock and she'd released her wedding dress, she almost tripped.

She'd never forgotten the irony of her name. She'd been named Gracie, and she was the least graceful person to walk the earth. That's how it felt most days, at least.

She tried to pull herself together and straighten her skirt as she turned toward the man. "What now?"

Dillon watched her, almost with a hint of amusement in his eyes. The spark of humor quickly disappeared as he nodded toward his horse. "Now we're going to take a little ride."

Her shoulders tensed. "But there are no cars out here."

He looked again at the stallion waiting at the water's edge. "I hope you like horses."

———

DILLON CLIMBED onto Blaze before reaching for the woman. She hadn't shared her name yet, and he guessed that was on purpose. He'd find out soon enough.

Bridezilla stared up at the horse, her lips twisting into a frown as if she had no idea what to do with either him or his horse.

"Put your foot into the stirrup," Dillon directed.

She tried to do as he said, but she still couldn't seem to figure out how to get on the horse.

"Your other foot," Dillon directed, amusement lacing his voice.

She harrumphed before raising her wedding dress up just slightly and sliding her bare foot into the stirrup as he directed.

Dillon took her hand and boosted her onto the saddle behind him.

He didn't normally like having two people on his stallion but, in this situation, it was going to have to work.

Thankfully, they could cut through the woods and they'd be at the Community Safety building relatively quickly.

He knew his stallion was strong and could handle the extra weight. Besides, this woman's dress probably weighed more than she did. She was a tiny thing—a tiny thing with a good dose of fight in her gaze.

"You're going to want to hold on," Dillon instructed.

The woman hesitated a moment before putting her hands on either side of his waist.

"You're going to want to hold on tighter," he told her.

Dillon could appreciate that the woman was being cautious. But this was no time for that. The last thing he needed was for her to bounce right off Blaze.

Finally, the woman's grip tightened. Once she was secure, Dillon nudged his horse, and they began trotting through the sand.

Ordinarily, he'd try to skirt around these woods and all the hazards they posed—everything from wild animals to quicksand. For today, Dillon needed to take the quickest route back to the station.

He directed his horse into the dense forest that comprised a thousand acres of their little eight thousand-acre island. He knew a path that would be a shortcut. But most of this maritime forest was too thick to traverse.

"So, what's your name?" Dillon asked as they moseyed through the woods.

"I'd rather not say."

"You know you're going to have to tell me when we get to the station," he reminded her. Bridezilla was just delaying the inevitable.

"Well, we're not at the station yet."

He fought another smile. The woman tried to sound tough, but Dillon knew it was only to cover up her vulnerability.

His curiosity continued to grow.

He couldn't wait to find out this woman's story.

The guys at the station would love hearing about today's rescue.

"There's a horse up there!" She gasped and pointed in the distance.

"That's right. That's Rocky, one of our wild horses here on the island."

"That's . . . amazing. Wild horses? I dreamed about seeing those as a child, ever since I read *Misty of Chincoteague*."

"You've come to the right place then."

"Where's the rest of his herd?"

"Rocky is actually what we call a lone stallion," Dillon explained. "Another stallion took over his harem—that's what they're called out in nature—so now he's destined to live out the rest of his days alone."

"That sounds . . . sad."

Dillon shrugged. It didn't actually sound that bad to Dillon. In fact, he thought of himself as a lone stallion. He'd been burned by love once, and he had no desire to put himself in that situation again.

It was the single life for him from now until forever, and he was more than okay with that.

He nodded to Rocky as they passed. The horse continued to chew on some acorns. The food wasn't normally what horses ate—not domesticated ones, at least. But the wild horses had adapted to life on this island. Persimmons and sea oats were on their menu of choice.

The animals had proven they could survive. They'd been here on Cape Corral for hundreds of years now.

As Dillon stared at Rocky another moment, something shifted behind him.

The next instant, the woman leapt from the back of the horse. With more skill than Dillon assumed she had, she hit the ground and rolled. Just as quickly, she popped to her feet and began darting through the forest.

Dillon let out a breath as dread filled him.

He should have figured this was too easy.

Now he was going to have to catch her.

CHAPTER FIVE

GRACIE WASN'T THINKING. She was acting on instinct—*survival* instinct. Before, she had buried the fight inside her, settling for permissiveness instead.

Not anymore.

Her mind had rushed through all the possibilities for escape as she'd been riding with the cowboy to the police station.

Her thoughts stopped at one realization: she couldn't sit in a jail cell.

Constantine would find her. He'd force her to go back with him.

And he was charming enough to convince people that he was trustworthy.

He always did.

The man had used that charm to convince Gracie they should get married.

Thank goodness, she'd come to her senses before it was too late.

Branches slapped her arms, briars tugged at her skirt, and roots scratched her bare feet as she sprinted through the forest. She didn't care.

As Gracie stared ahead of her, she knew she couldn't remain on the sandy path cutting through the forest. If she wanted to escape, she had to duck into the thick foliage and go deeper into this maritime wilderness.

The cowboy and his horse couldn't fit through the deep confines of these gnarled woods that reminded her of a twisted fairy tale.

"Stop!" Dillon yelled behind her. "You don't know what you're doing."

Gracie kept running.

The man was blowing smoke, trying to slow her down. It wouldn't look good for the fire chief to tell his colleagues that he'd let a woman in his custody get away from him.

But she couldn't risk going with him.

Gracie ducked low, knowing that she was going

to have a new challenge in front of her as she attempted this escape.

Her wedding dress slowed her down. She heard the fabric rip as she pushed through the thick landscape.

She didn't care.

This dress would be ruined, and it wouldn't cause Gracie to lose a single second of sleep. Too many bad memories were associated with it.

She just needed to move.

Her life depended on it.

Gracie ducked and turned as the trees pushed closer.

She knew the cowboy was close behind.

He'd jumped from his horse and had taken off after her. She heard his footsteps.

She couldn't lose any time by looking behind her to check how near he was.

The only advantage Gracie had was her size. She was significantly smaller than the man. That would allow her to maneuver between these trees.

But her dress was a huge disadvantage. Gracie had gotten rid of the train when she'd abandoned her car, but the skirt was full and overwhelming. Constantine had insisted she have the dress designed for her. Had even called her royalty.

A clearing appeared ahead.

Maybe this was her chance to gain some ground.

But as soon as Gracie stepped through the trees, the ground disappeared beneath her.

For the second time today, she found herself falling into the unknown.

DILLON SAW Bridezilla disappear and gritted his teeth.

He'd tried to warn the woman about the dangers of these woods.

She was obviously headstrong—and desperate.

The forest around them had formed over old sand dunes. Most of the land in this coastal part of North Carolina was relatively flat. But out here in Wash Woods, there were hills, cliffs, and hollows.

It felt like a miniature version of the Blue Ridge Mountains. The sight still perplexed Dillon at times. It was just one more thing that made this area intriguing.

Dillon dove toward the woman as he saw her falling.

He caught her wrist as she went over the cliff.

She let out a grunt as her body jolted to a stop and dangled midair.

As Dillon glanced down at the woman, he flinched at what he saw.

A small, swampy pond stagnated below her.

A water moccasin coiled on one of the logs near the bottom.

"I don't need your help," Bridezilla said through clenched teeth.

The desperation in her green eyes belied her words.

How long were they going to have to play this game? Dillon hadn't exactly signed up for this when he'd agreed to fill in for Levi.

Dillon fought a sigh before saying, "I beg to differ."

"The water would have broken my fall."

"Which would have been reason to celebrate . . . until that water moccasin found you."

The woman glanced down and gasped as the snake came into sight. When she looked back up at Dillon, the fear in her gaze was unmistakable. Maybe the severity of the situation was finally getting through to her.

"Are you going to cooperate now?" Dillon didn't try to keep the dry tone from his voice.

The woman stared up at him another moment.

She still wasn't convinced?

Unbelievable.

Against his better judgment, Dillon loosened his grip. The woman's hand began to slide.

She gasped again and tried to clasp her fingers tightly around his.

Dillon hid his smile, not letting on that he'd done that on purpose.

Then Dillon waited for her to change her mind.

Her revelation should be coming at any second now.

Three.

Two.

One—

"Yes, I'll cooperate," Bridezilla rushed. "I promise. Just don't drop me. Please."

Dillon climbed on his knees and pulled until the woman landed on the ground beside him.

As she glanced up, sand covered one side of her exquisite face.

Despite her dress, the woman managed to wrench herself to her feet and wipe the granules from her cheeks. Her gaze hesitantly fluttered toward his, her expression a mix of a scowling irritation and overwhelming gratitude.

"Thank you." She seemed to force herself to say the words as she addressed him.

"You can thank me by cooperating." Dillon had a feeling that wouldn't be happening, though.

This woman was stubborn and headstrong.

And he couldn't play Mr. Nice Guy anymore.

Dillon pulled the handcuffs from his belt and grabbed the woman. "I didn't want to have to do this."

Before she could fight him, he pulled her wrists in front of her and fastened her hands together.

She gasped as she stared at the silver now adorning her wrists. It probably wasn't the kind of ring she'd envisioned for the day.

"Is this really necessary?" she asked, her lips parting in disbelief.

"Apparently, yes. It is."

"I thought you were a firefighter. Do firefighters around here always carry handcuffs? How do I know you're not some kind of psycho?"

The woman had a point. But her argument wasn't going to work. "I'm also a backup law enforcement officer. It's your lucky day."

"My lucky day?" The woman's eyes narrowed as she let out a bitter chuckle. "You have no idea."

What did that mean?

Dillon would find out soon enough.

Because Bridezilla was going to need to provide him with some answers as soon as they got back to the station.

CHAPTER SIX

GRACIE DIDN'T FIGHT as Dillon helped her onto the horse. This time, he didn't ride with her. Instead, he took the reins and led the stallion through the forest—probably so he could keep an eye on her.

Gracie supposed she didn't stand a chance of trying to escape again.

She fought a frown.

It was just as well. She wasn't cut out to make it in a place like this. The only jungle she knew how to navigate was the urban one. Even that one had its challenges.

She fought tears as she resigned herself to whatever was to come.

Arrested.

Charged.

Jailed.

Gracie had no idea what would happen after that. How long could she be sentenced for stealing that boat?

Still, she'd rather go to prison than marry Constantine. That was the only thought that provided her any consolation.

"You want to tell me your name yet?" Dillon asked as they ambled along through the woods.

As the man's voice cut into her thoughts, Gracie jerked her head toward him.

He looked so calm, so in control. Even after what she'd done, he'd never shown a moment of being frazzled or uncertain.

A moment of envy shot through her. Gracie felt anything but calm. She felt like she wanted to start running, with no idea where she was going.

While carrying scissors.

With dish soap on the floor.

With her hair down, blustering in the autumn breeze until the locks were unruly and obscuring her vision.

In fact, that was exactly what she'd done—minus the scissors and dish soap.

"Gracie," she finally muttered as the man's question hung in the air.

"Gracie? That's a pretty name."

She shrugged. "It fits my life, especially the fact that it's one big contradiction."

Dillon glanced at her but didn't say anything else.

For some reason, she decided to fill the silence anyway. "For starters, I'm the least graceful person you'll ever meet."

Dillon still said nothing, so she continued.

"My parents tried to enroll me in ballet classes, and the teacher actually kicked me out. That's how hopeless I was."

A small smile tugged at his lips.

"I made the cheerleading squad in high school," she said, adding one last story. "I was at the top of the pyramid and fell off. It's still played on YouTube to this day on 'how not to be a cheerleader' videos. They call that move 'The Gracie.'"

He still didn't openly react to what she said.

Was he just being nice? Did he not have a sense of humor?

Instead of responding, he asked, "What brings you to Cape Corral?"

Gracie glanced at him again, wondering if there was any way to get out of this conversation. Hadn't she already shared enough? She'd told him the cheerleading story, for goodness sake!

"Do I have to tell you?" She licked her lips. "Is this a part of my interrogation or can I keep private things private?"

Dillon studied her for a moment, contemplation flashing through his eyes. "I suppose it's not essential that you tell me that information."

That was all Gracie needed to hear. She clamped her mouth shut.

The less he knew, the better.

The less *anyone* knew, the better.

She needed to remember that if she was going to get through this situation . . . and remain alive.

DILLON DIDN'T KNOW why something about the woman entertained him.

But there was more to his impression of her than that.

He saw the unmistakable fear lining the woman's gaze also.

His curiosity grew as he wondered what had led her to this area.

But Gracie obviously wasn't ready to talk about it.

They reached the Community Safety building, which housed both Fire and Rescue and the Forestry Division. The Forestry Division employed the law enforcement officers on the island, who were tasked for caring for both the people and the horses.

Dillon took his horse into the stable before helping Gracie slide from the saddle.

Just as she'd self-deprecatingly described the irony of her name, the woman nearly stumbled as her bare feet reached the ground.

Dillon caught her before she fell, his arms cupping her elbows as she lunged toward him.

Her dress bunched between them, billowing with the breeze at the sudden motion.

The woman was a sight for sore eyes, as the saying went. Feisty. Dainty. Headstrong.

And obviously in trouble.

Mud covered one of her thin arms. Leaves were caught in her hair. She'd lost one dangly earring.

But her obvious beauty still shone through. Any hot-blooded male could see it.

Dillon cleared his throat and stepped back, unsure why his thoughts had gone there.

"Colby," he called to one of his guys who worked

in the distance. "You mind putting Blaze away for me?"

"No problem, Boss."

Colby strode toward them, grabbed his horse's reins, and led Blaze inside the stall. As he did, Dillon took Gracie's arm and accompanied her into the cedar-sided building where his office was located. A small interrogation room was set up at the back.

Dillon briefly considered bypassing it or handing this woman off to Grant, who had more experience with these kinds of things.

But he changed his mind.

Grant was occupied at a meeting this afternoon. Dillon didn't want to spare the woman the full experience of being arrested.

Being in the interrogation room would be good for her. She had no clue just how much trouble she'd gotten herself into. She didn't seem like the type to easily learn these things either.

As soon as they stepped into the gray room with the stark walls, Dillon pointed to a seat across the table. Gracie didn't budge. Instead, she raised her wrists.

"Can you take these things off, at least?" she asked. "I don't think I'm going to overpower you."

The woman had a point. As Dillon reached for her hands, he noticed the tremble there.

She was nervous.

Good.

Seeing something other than the defiance she'd displayed earlier was a positive sign.

Gracie rubbed her wrists as she took a seat.

Dillon sat across from her and leaned back in the chair. He would start as laid-back Dillon. But if he had to, he'd transform into intense Dillon. He could play both good cop and bad cop.

This woman wasn't totally innocent. She'd stolen a boat and tried to resist arrest. Both of those charges were serious.

"Now, do you want to tell me what's going on?" Dillon started, his gaze locking with hers.

Gracie shrugged, her pert features scrunching with regret. "Not really."

"Let's try again." He let out a sigh, wondering why she had to make things so complicated. "Why did you steal that boat?"

"It's like I said, I didn't want to take it for good. I only wanted to borrow it." Her lips tugged down in a frown.

"To do what? Take it for a joyride?"

Gracie seemed to consider his words before

offering a half shrug. "In so many words, yes. I wanted to take it on a joyride."

He pointed to her wedding dress. "And what about your gown? Care to explain?"

She glanced down as if suddenly remembering what she wore. "Oh, this old thing? It was for a . . . costume party."

"A costume party in Cape Corral?" Dillon felt confident that was *not* what she was doing.

"I think I got turned around. I was confused. *Very* confused."

This woman was full of it. But Dillon knew there was more to her story. He just wasn't sure what it would take to get to the heart of the matter.

He didn't want to throw this woman in jail.

But he would if he had to.

Because, as far as he was concerned, no one was above the law.

Not even this firecracker of a woman with the ironic first name.

CHAPTER SEVEN

GRACIE'S MIND RACED. She had to think of a way out of this. She couldn't go to jail.

She was a survivor. She always had been.

That couldn't change now.

But as she stared at Dillon McGrath, she knew she wouldn't be changing the man's mind. He was clearly irritated with her and clearly determined to teach her a lesson.

She'd dealt with scarier men than this brute, however.

Gracie crossed her arms and leaned back, a chill washing over her. Maybe it was this stark gray room. Maybe it was the fact she'd been drenched and her dress still retained some dampness. Maybe it was the situation.

Either way, she nearly felt feverish she was so chilled.

"So, I'm facing charges of stealing a boat?" She raised her chin, determined not to show weakness.

Dillon's expression remained placid and unemotional. "That's right."

"And I'm facing these charges because the owner of the boat filed a police report and pressed charges against me." Another question jarred her. "Have any reports about the missing boat gone public? Been on the news?"

Dillon's eyes narrowed, as if he hadn't expected her question. "Not that I know of. I suppose the media has more important things to report on."

She released her breath. That was good news, at least. If Constantine heard about the missing boat, he might put things together. He might realize that Gracie had driven south from the church where they were supposed to marry.

Even though Gracie abandoned her car in the woods, it was only a matter of time before someone found it. Still, she needed to buy as much time as she could.

No doubt, Constantine was out there now looking for her. He'd probably employed his minions to help him.

She was too valuable to him to slip away so easily without any kind of fight.

"The owner of the boat has filed a police report," Dillon said. "He hasn't pressed charges. Not yet."

Gracie's heart lifted with hope. Maybe it wasn't too late to make things right. Maybe she still had hope of escaping.

"Do you think I could talk to him?"

Dillon's eyes narrowed. "Talk to whom?"

"The owner of the boat."

"Why would you do that?" A knot formed between the man's eyes, and he looked truly perplexed.

"I want to plead my case."

The knot disappeared, replaced with a smirk. "You really think that will work?"

Gracie shrugged, unaffected by the doubt in his voice. "I think it can't hurt to have a conversation."

Dillon stared at her another moment before nodding and straightening. "Fine. I'll let you talk to Mr. Dunleavy."

"Perfect. Thank you." Maybe this would work. Gracie could hope.

Dillon dialed a number on his phone, muttered a few things into the mouthpiece, and then handed the device to Gracie with a smile that looked a little too satisfied. "Have at it."

She drew in a deep breath and tried to quickly form what she would say.

She rose to her feet and paced toward the corner before beginning the conversation.

A few minutes later, Gracie turned toward Dillon, feeling a surge of triumph. "Good news! Mr. Dunleavy said I could pay him back for the wear and tear on the boat, as well as gas, and he wouldn't press charges."

"What?" Dillon stared at her in disbelief.

Gracie nodded. "It's true. Isn't that great?"

Dillon glowered down at her before taking the phone to confirm her words were true.

"YOU SWEET-TALKED THE MAN, didn't you?" Dillon shook his head in disbelief as he put his phone back into his pocket.

Gracie was one of those women who had power over people, wasn't she? She could charm her way in and out of situations. She used her sweet smile and friendly voice to get what she wanted.

That was one more reason not to like her.

Gracie shrugged, her eyes a little too innocent as she stared at him from across the table. "I don't know what you're talking about."

"You used that sugary voice of yours to get your way." He shook his head and leaned back. "I should have known."

She raised her hands as if innocent. "What I did was apologize profusely and said I wasn't in my right mind at the time. If my voice was sweet, it's because God made it that way."

There she went again, trying to use her charms . . .

"And Mr. Dunleavy told you that you could pay him for the wear and tear of the boat, and he wouldn't press charges?"

Gracie shrugged. "What can I say? Walter sounds like a very kind man. Very understanding."

"I've met Walter Dunleavy before, and he is anything but nice and kind." This woman knew how to work people. That fact got under Dillon's skin.

"You're not going to try to make him change his mind, are you?" Alarm charged through her voice as if the realization shook her up.

The idea was tempting, but Dillon shook his head. "No, I'm not going to do that. But I'm very curious how you plan to pay him back. You don't have a wallet or phone with you."

Some of the hopefulness disappeared from her gaze. "I'm going to need to figure that out, aren't I?"

"Yes, you are." Dillon was curious to see how she would get out of this one.

Gracie nibbled on her bottom lip for a moment before looking up at him. "You don't know anyone who needs any help around here, do you? To the tune of . . . somewhere around one hundred fifty dollars?"

Dillon narrowed his eyes before shrugging. "I can't say I do."

Her hopeful smile completely vanished. "There's got to be something I can do."

That's when an idea hit him. "There is *one* thing that might earn you some money. If you're interested."

"Yes, I am! I'll do anything." She leaned toward him and waited to hear what the job might be.

Dillon smiled. This was going to be fun.

And maybe it would teach Gracie No-Last-Name a lesson about being on the wrong side of crime.

CHAPTER EIGHT

GRACIE FROWNED as she lifted the pitchfork and shook it, trying to separate the horse manure from the wood shavings and hay.

Mucking horse stalls? *This* was how Dillon McGrath wanted her to earn money?

She sighed, the air from her lungs blowing her hair from her face as she stabbed some more straw. The scent of horse manure, salty air, and dusty hay rose around her.

She sneezed.

Then sneezed again.

And again.

Great. Was she allergic to hay? Wouldn't that just be the icing on today's already rotten cake?

Amazingly, Dillon had found some old jeans and

a sweatshirt left at the station that Gracie could wear. She'd donned some cowboy boots that had also been left there, and she'd pulled her hair back into a ponytail—most of her hair, at least. Several rebellious tendrils escaped.

Thankfully, there were no mirrors for Gracie to see herself. She was sure she wouldn't like the image she saw there.

It was just as well.

She wouldn't be staying here in Cape Corral for long.

Hopefully, after today, she wouldn't have to see Dillon McGrath again.

Ever.

The man was infuriating. It didn't matter if she tried to comply with his wishes, he still seemed unaffected by her. It was only when Gracie wasn't trying to be charming that he looked halfway amused.

Her eyes narrowed again as she lifted more horse poop from the stall and put it into a wheelbarrow. Despite how non-ideal this situation was, she'd still rather be doing this than marrying Constantine right now.

She glanced at her watch. Actually, the two of them would have been at their reception at the ritzy ballroom just outside of DC right now. She'd be forced under duress to pretend she was happy.

But she wouldn't have been.

Not knowing her uncle's life was on the line.

She shuddered as she remembered all of it.

Mostly, Gracie remembered the fear.

The complete and utter fear.

She'd been only thirty minutes away from making the biggest mistake of her life. Thank goodness, she'd happened to walk past that room at the church when she did. Thank goodness, she'd seen the truth.

She hadn't hesitated to grab her keys and purse, sneak out the back door of the building, and jump into her car.

Then she'd driven. And driven.

Four hours, to be exact. Until Gracie's car had finally run out of gas. She'd hidden the vehicle in the woods and searched for a way to keep running.

That's when she'd stumbled across Mr. Dunleavy's boat floating near a dock on the sound.

No one had been around.

Taking it had seemed like a good idea at the time.

When the skiff had actually started, she'd seen it as a sign.

Maybe Gracie should just run again. After all, she needed to keep moving. That was the best way to ensure Constantine didn't find her. She was wasting valuable time right now—time she should be using to put more distance between herself and the man of her nightmares.

Yet Gracie wanted to be a woman of her word.

She frowned and nibbled on her bottom lip.

As she did, she glanced around.

Running *was* tempting.

But Gracie had agreed to do this work, she reminded herself again. It was only fair that she followed through.

Even if the task was humiliating.

But she needed to start thinking. Needed to start planning.

Once this job was finished, she was out of here.

She needed to figure out where she would go and how she would get there.

Her life depended on it.

DILLON GLANCED at his phone and felt his jaw harden.

Lauren had sent him a text message . . . a picture of her with her new husband.

He gritted his teeth as he looked at her smiling face in the photo.

Had Lauren sent this just to rub it in how happy she was without him?

Most likely.

When she'd left him after two years of marriage, Dillon had done everything in his power to win her back.

Nothing had worked.

And now she'd moved on.

Permanently.

He should be happy for her.

But the two of them were supposed to have forever together.

Lauren hadn't kept up her end of the bargain.

The one thing Dillon knew for certain was that he never ever wanted to put himself in that position again. As far as he was concerned, it was the single road for him from here on out.

He slid his phone back into his pocket as Grant walked into the stable.

Grant paused and stared at Gracie as she worked in the stall in the distance before narrowing his eyes. "Who is that? Do I want to ask?"

"Probably not." Dillon crossed his arms and watched Gracie work, fighting the utter amusement the sight brought. The woman definitely wasn't the stall-mucking type.

Which made this even better.

The experience would be a nice lesson in humility for the pampered princess.

"I heard about your rescue." Grant glanced at him. "Is it true the woman was wearing a wedding dress when you pulled her out of the water?"

Dillon rubbed his jaw and nodded as he remembered the ordeal. Colby must have told Grant about it. Dillon had briefed him as Gracie was getting changed. Colby had also kept an eye on the woman as Dillon changed into some dry clothes.

"That's right," Dillon said. "Her designer dress nearly killed her."

"That's a first. What's her story?"

He shrugged. "I don't know. She didn't tell me, and I couldn't force any details out of her."

"That's the woman, isn't it?" Grant nodded toward Gracie, realization dawning in his voice. "You put her to work?"

"It's a long story. Believe me. But this is good for her—she just doesn't know it yet."

Grant clucked his tongue as he twisted his head.

"Well, I look forward to hearing all the rigmarole one day. You need anything from me?"

"Not right now," Dillon said. "I'm just overseeing our ward at the moment."

"Is she staying on the island overnight?"

Dillon shrugged. He hadn't thought that far ahead. One thing at a time—and that one thing, right now, was paying Mr. Dunleavy back.

"I don't know what she'll do tonight," Dillon finally said. "Is there any room at the inn?"

"I heard it was full again this weekend. Lots of fishermen in town."

Dillon mentally groaned. Where *would* this woman stay if she couldn't leave Cape Corral? It was getting too late to go anywhere else. He couldn't exactly send her out on her own—not knowing there was no housing available and that she had no money with her.

He would figure something out.

There was always the jail cell, if nothing else.

Grant clutched Dillon's shoulder, not bothering to hide the humor in his voice. "Good luck, my friend. Good luck."

As Grant walked away, Dillon heard Gracie grunt. He paced toward her to see how she was doing.

He fought a smile when he saw her struggling with the pitchfork. Then again, maybe he should be really careful right now.

That pitchfork could be dangerous if Gracie wanted it to be.

She looked back at him and scowled. "Are you happy now?"

Dillon shrugged and leaned on the open stall door, crossing his flannel-clad arms. "Nothing to be happy about. I'm just double-checking your work."

"Cracking the whip, so to speak?" She scowled again. "I'll have you know that I have a great work ethic, thank you. And I will get this done, if it's the last thing I do today."

Something about the woman's feistiness intrigued him. "Good to know."

He heard another footstep behind him and turned, fully expecting to see Grant there again.

Instead, a man Dillon had never seen before stepped into the stable.

As he did, Gracie gripped Dillon's arm.

Gripped it hard.

Her nails dug into him, and Dillon felt the woman leaning into his back, almost as if . . . hiding?

Had she lost her mind?

He glanced at her and saw something glimmering in her eyes—all her smugness gone.

"Please," she whispered. "Don't tell him I'm here. Please."

Concern stretched taut across his shoulders.

What was going on? There was definitely more to Gracie's story.

CHAPTER NINE

GRACIE COULD HARDLY BREATHE as fear pounded through her.

How had Constantine found her here?

And the even bigger question . . . would Dillon sell her out?

Clearly, the fire chief didn't care for her. Maybe he was just looking for the chance to get rid of her. Or to find out more information about what was going on.

Gracie had no idea. She didn't know the brute well enough to trust him.

But however Dillon responded would determine her future.

He couldn't possibly have any idea the power he held right now.

She pressed herself into the wall of the stall, hoping that Constantine wouldn't come any closer. Praying that the man didn't see her.

How had he even tracked her this far? How was it possible? Not enough time had passed.

"Can I help you?" Dillon called.

Gracie held her breath as she waited to hear what would play out.

"I'm looking for someone." Constantine's familiar, deep voice rang through the air, and nausea pooled in her stomach. "A woman named Gracie Loveland. I heard that you were on duty today, and I should talk to you."

"Gracie Loveland?" Dillon repeated. "Is there a reason I may have come across this woman?"

"I heard rumors she was headed this way. I hoped that in a place this small, you might have seen her."

Gracie's head began to spin again as she waited to hear how Dillon would respond. She couldn't go back with Constantine. Her future depended on it.

"I wish I could help you. But I can't. I'm sorry."

Relief filled her.

He hadn't sold her out.

Not yet.

"It's okay." Constantine's deep voice filled the air. "I just thought I heard you talking to someone."

"Just my horse."

"Of course. It was worth a shot."

"If you give me your information, I can call you if I hear anything."

Gracie waited to hear what Constantine would say. She prayed he didn't come any closer. That he didn't see her.

Fear churned inside her with enough force she thought she might puke.

"That's okay," her ex-fiancé finally said. "I'm probably not going to be staying in town long."

"You came all this way just to see if you could find her?" A new curiosity entered Dillon's voice, even though his body language remained casual. "It's not easy to get to the island with the bridge washed out."

"Those are true words." Constantine let out a chuckle, but the sound quickly faded. "But it's urgent that I find her."

"Why is that?" Dillon shifted. "Is there something I should know?"

Gracie's heart pounded in her ears, each thrum tightening her lungs.

"She's not in her right mind." Constantine lowered his voice as if confiding in a friend. "I'm afraid that she's a danger not only to herself . . . but to others."

Gracie's mouth dropped open. Had Constantine really just said that?

Her fear turned to anger, and she fisted her hands at her side.

How dare he? Constantine was manipulating this situation to make her look bad!

"I'll keep that in mind," Dillon said. "Good luck finding her."

With these final words, footsteps padded from the stable.

Gracie was safe.

For now.

She knew that she owed Dillon an explanation.

But she dreaded sharing any details with him.

AS SOON AS the man disappeared from sight, Dillon took Gracie's arm and pulled her deeper into the stall and out of sight.

"Do you want to tell me what's going on now?"

he whispered, making sure his body blocked her from anyone who might return. It wasn't hard, considering he probably had a hundred pounds on her.

Dillon felt the tremble rushing through Gracie's muscles as she stared up at him. For a moment, she looked more like a little girl than the headstrong woman he'd met earlier.

"Not really." Her voice cracked and any snarkiness was gone from her gaze.

There was only fear now. Stark, raw fear.

Dillon's gut clenched. He'd gotten a bad vibe from the man who'd come looking for her. Beneath the guy's suave motions and words, Dillon sensed a control freak.

And his claim that Gracie was a danger to herself and others?

Well, she might be a danger to herself . . . but not on purpose.

There was more to this story.

Gracie licked her lips and looked up at Dillon, something changing in her gaze.

"Look, you've done a lot for me," she started. "But . . . my situation is complicated. I'm not sure you want to know the details."

This woman was scared for her life, Dillon realized. That's why she'd been on that boat.

She'd been running away.

But just what was her relationship with this guy? Romantic? Professional? Accidental?

"Why don't you let me help you?" He locked gazes with her, determined to drive home the point that he was serious.

Gracie's eyes widened. "You'd help me? After everything I've done?"

"I know a woman in trouble when I see one. And I don't like bullies. My gut tells me that's exactly what that man who just came in here is—maybe even worse than a bully."

Her wide eyes probed his as if trying to gauge the sincerity of his words.

"I'll tell you . . . but not here," she finally whispered. "Not now. I'm afraid he's going to come back. He's . . . he's underhanded like that."

Dillon nodded. Suddenly, it didn't matter if Gracie finished her work here.

Dillon would be paying her out of his own pocket, so, as far as he was concerned, she'd earned what she needed.

While she finished this last stall, Dillon would keep a lookout for that man again.

But a bad feeling brewed in his stomach.

There was far more to Gracie's story . . . and based on the sense of danger Dillon had felt around that man, things might go from bad to worse.

CHAPTER TEN

GRACIE HAD INSISTED she finish mucking the stalls, even though Dillon had told her she could stop.

But she could hardly concentrate as she got back to work.

Gracie kept expecting Constantine to appear again. For him to see her. To demand she go with him.

She could hardly breathe when she considered that prospect.

How was she ever going to escape from this man's clutches? Was it even a possibility? Or should she just succumb to the inevitable?

Becoming his wife.

Handing everything her family had worked for over to him.

Living life uncertain of when he might snap and kill her.

She couldn't willingly live that way. She was stronger than that. More of a fighter.

Gracie couldn't forget that truth, no matter what happened.

She'd humble herself, even if it meant trusting Dillon McGrath.

For now, she needed to finish up here.

She felt Dillon's eyes on her as she worked. She was determined to save face, to prove to him that she was capable, responsible, and a woman of her word.

Another part of her felt better knowing the imposing man was near. Something about him screamed strength and made him seem like the type people didn't mess with.

He'd already proven that, hadn't he?

Finally, Gracie finished and wiped her brow with the sleeve of her blue sweatshirt.

This work wasn't for the faint of heart. But the horses were nice. She'd talked to them in between cleaning each stall, and they were great company—plus, they didn't nose into her past.

She had so many questions about this place.

But this wasn't the time to ask.

Not yet.

Dillon straightened and strode toward her as she stepped from the last stall. "All done?"

"You want to check my work?"

Gracie fully expected him to say yes and to revel in any mistakes she'd made. Instead, he shook his head.

"No, I watched you," he said. "You did fine."

She nodded, trying not to show her surprise—or her pleasure—at his approval. "That's . . . great."

Dillon paused long enough to rub Blaze's nose. The horse leaned his head into Dillon's hand, and the man's features softened for a moment.

"You deserve an extra carrot tonight," he murmured. "I'll make sure you get one, okay?"

Gracie's heart softened for a minute as she watched Dillon with his horse. Maybe he wasn't as tough as she'd first assumed. The man *did* have a soft side.

But she knew she couldn't avoid talking to him forever.

She only hoped she didn't regret this.

"WE SHOULD GO INTO MY OFFICE." Dillon turned toward Gracie, anxious to hear about how she knew that man.

Gracie glanced at the door leading from the stable, her gaze clouding with fear. "Okay, but . . ."

Dillon waited for her to finish. When she didn't, he asked, "But what?"

The fear in her gaze nearly spilled over. "Can you make sure Constantine is really gone? He can't see me, Dillon. He can't know I'm here. Please."

Dillon had so many questions. But he didn't ask them. Not yet.

"Stay here while I check." He strode to the door of the stable and peered out.

No one was there.

That he could see.

He scanned everything once more.

Some cars were parked at the inn next door.

Could that man be inside one of them?

Dillon squinted. It was hard to say. Some of the windows were tinted. Plus, it was getting dark outside.

Based on Gracie's body language, he needed to proceed with caution.

He turned back around, halfway expecting to

find Gracie gone, that she'd taken the opportunity to run.

But she was still there.

Still waiting.

Still scared.

Dillon made a split-second decision.

"Pull up your hood," he told her as he strode closer.

"What?" She squinted.

"Just do it." He paused before adding, "Please."

Gracie hesitated only a moment before pulling the sweatshirt hood over her head.

The oversized clothing concealed her petite frame.

But that wouldn't be enough.

"Let's go out the back. I'll take you into the station through the rear of the building."

She nodded.

Dillon took his jacket off and draped it over her shoulders. Then he led her out the back. He slipped an arm around her waist and urged her to go faster.

As they walked, Dillon looked around, looked for signs of anyone.

An open, sandy pasture surrounded by a wooden fence stared back. Behind that stood some trees. In the far distance were several houses.

He saw nothing and no one out of the ordinary.

Finally, they reached the back door, and Dillon ushered her inside, locking the door behind him.

Gracie released a breath as she turned toward him once within the safe confines of the building. "Thank you."

She slipped off his coat and handed it back to him.

"It's no problem." Dillon took her arm. "Now, let's go to my office and talk. Really talk."

He needed to know what he was getting into before this went any further.

CHAPTER ELEVEN

THINGS WEREN'T SUPPOSED to work out like this.

He had a plan.

That plan did *not* include Gracie Loveland running away.

He had to find her.

He would do whatever was necessary to accomplish that.

And if he couldn't force her into marriage, there were other ways to get what he wanted.

More *painful* ways.

But he wasn't opposed to those possibilities.

Gracie was around here somewhere.

He knew it in his gut. He'd traced the GPS on her car. He'd set that precaution in place long ago.

After he found her abandoned car, he headed toward the shore and learned a boat had been stolen. This was a logical place for her to head.

He was determined to find her, and no one would get in the way of his plans.

No one.

He would keep searching. Eventually, he'd track Gracie down.

And when he did, she would pay for what she'd done.

A smile stretched across his face at the thought.

He would enjoy watching her suffer.

Maybe he'd even enjoy it a little too much.

His hands fisted at his side.

It was just a matter of time until he could experience that satisfaction.

CHAPTER TWELVE

GRACIE DREW in a deep breath as she sat across from Dillon in his office. He'd closed the door and waited patiently—which almost made all this worse.

The silence was horrible. And haunting. And filled her with dread.

Gracie didn't want to tell this man the truth. The truth was humiliating. Painful. Sad.

But if Gracie wanted Dillon's help, then she had no choice.

Given the fact she had no money, no car, and no place to stay, it might be wise to have someone on her side—at least until she could get out of town.

She rubbed her hands on her jeans as she stared at the man who'd twice rescued her. Keeping the story to herself was easy. It made it seem more like a nightmare than reality.

Speaking it out loud . . . the act would make her relive those horrible moments she'd rather forget. She drew in a deep breath, trying to draw on her last ounce of strength.

"I was supposed to get married today," she finally started, dread pooling in her stomach.

An eyebrow flickered up. "I gathered that."

"But I couldn't go through with it. So I ran, and I ended up here." That was the short and sweet version. Would that be enough to satisfy Dillon? Probably not. But Gracie figured it was worth a shot, at least.

"Who was that man?" Dillon asked.

"He's Constantine DiMarzio. I was supposed to marry him."

Dillon shifted in his chair, his motions still as calm and cool as ever. "I'm going to need a few more details if you want me to help you."

Dread clutched Gracie. Dillon's words were true. She knew that. She just didn't want to go deeper.

She twirled a lock of hair as her thoughts raced. "Could I have some coffee first? Maybe it will help my headache. And I'm a little chilly—but I don't need to go to the clinic, if that's what you're thinking. Coffee . . . coffee is what I need."

"Of course." Dillon left the room long enough to get her a cup, along with a sandwich and fruit cup. "Someone brought some food by the station earlier. You're probably hungry."

Now that he mentioned it, Gracie was famished. She'd hardly eaten all day.

"Thank you." She opened the bowl of fruit and stabbed a grape with a plastic fork.

Gracie wished she could enjoy this. But she had too much on her mind. Maybe when she finished.

But probably not.

She was just delaying the inevitable right now.

She sucked in a deep breath and set the food back on the desk for later. "I met Constantine eight months ago, and we started dating. At first, he was . . . perfect. Eerily so, in retrospect. But, after a while, I noticed he had some controlling tendencies, not to mention a short fuse. I sensed there were things he wasn't telling me, that he wasn't being forthright about. I knew we weren't going to work, so I tried to break up."

"What happened?"

She licked her lips as the day flashed back into her mind. "He insisted we were meant to be together.

He dropped on one knee right there and proposed. He even had a ring with him."

"What did you say?"

"No, of course. My mind was made up, and a ring wasn't going to make me rethink things."

"But you were supposed to get married today . . ." Dillon said. "So something changed your mind."

"I'm getting to that." Gracie sucked in another breath. "I told Constantine no, but he wouldn't listen. He was insistent—almost panicky. I asked him why my words weren't getting through to him. That's when he changed from someone who seemed desperate to marry me to someone with vengeance in his eyes."

"Why was he so determined?"

Gracie nibbled on her bottom lip before continuing. "It's a long story. But my mom and dad owned White Star Media."

Dillon's face tightened. "I've heard of White Star . . ."

Most people had. The company not only had several magazines but also three popular websites, and they'd just acquired a radio station not long ago.

"My mom and dad died in a car accident when I was fourteen. When that happened, my father's best friend—I've always called him Uncle Max—raised me. But when I turn thirty, it's in my parents' will that I'll take over the company."

Dillon's eyes widened as understanding seemed to dawn on him. "When do you turn thirty?"

Gracie drew in another breath, trying to keep her emotions under control. "In two weeks."

More realization rolled over Dillon's face. "So this guy—Constantine—wanted to marry you so he could somehow gain control over that company? He did realize that you could say no, right?"

"He did. That's why he abducted Uncle Max."

Dillon's eyebrows shot up. "How did that change things?"

"He said if I didn't marry him, they'd kill Max. He sent me a picture of Max, tied up. Constantine let me talk to him on the phone. I've never heard Max like that, sounding so scared."

"Did you think about going to the police?"

"He said I couldn't. Not if I wanted Max to live." Her voice cracked.

Dillon shifted. "I don't understand, though. Even if you married this Constantine guy, how would that give him control over your parents' company? And why does he even want to control it so badly?"

Gracie wiped her hands across her jeans again as the stress of the past couple of months surfaced stronger than ever. "I think Constantine is trying to make me look crazy. After we married, he would say I'm incompetent and figure out a way to gain control of the company that way."

"It's a bit of a stretch, but I guess maybe he could make that work."

"If anyone can make it work, it's Constantine. He's pretty determined. And he's smart—too smart for his own good."

"And why does he want the company?"

"I think there's more than one reason. First, I thought it was the money. Constantine would have a nice life."

"But if he married you, he'd have that anyway."

"Which is why I think there's a bigger reason also. I think he wants to control the messages that get out there. His brother is in politics, and I think he wants to change the narrative."

"So it's about power?"

Gracie nodded. "I think it is."

Dillon released a long breath. "And that led to today?"

"That's right. I was at the church. Trying to pretend I was okay with all this." Gracie paused for long enough to drag in a shaky breath. "But I walked by one of the rooms where the men were getting ready. My uncle Max was in there. I heard him talking. He was in on this and only pretending to be abducted." Nausea roiled in her at the memory.

How could Max have betrayed her like this?

"Who are these men?" Dillon asked.

"Constantine, his brother Angelino, and his best friend, Percy."

"After you heard your uncle Max talking with them, that's when you ran?" Dillon asked.

"That's when I ran. I knew I couldn't do this. I had to escape, and running was the only thing I knew to do."

Dillon nodded slowly.

Gracie waited, anxious to hear what he would say. She hadn't told anyone this. She didn't know whom she could trust.

If Max was plotting against her, then who else in her inner circle might be also?

That question would always haunt her.

***

DILLON TRIED to let what Gracie had told him sink in.

The story was . . . big. Outlandish. Unbelievable.

But he sensed the woman was telling the truth.

He couldn't even imagine going through what she had.

Now it made sense why she looked so skittish.

The question was, what should Dillon do about it? How could he help her?

Because there was no way he could hear Gracie's story and then send her out to fend for herself. It was clear she'd have trouble trusting anyone from her past, especially after being betrayed like she had.

"I don't know what to do." Gracie's gaze fluttered up to his. "If Constantine finds me, he's going to try to force me to marry him. He wants my parents' company, and he's made it clear that nothing—and no one—will get in his way."

"You think he'll continue to try to find ways to coerce you into doing what he wants?"

"I do." Gracie nodded. "Who else will Constantine and his guys abduct? Maybe they'll *really* abduct someone this time. Maybe they'll really *hurt* someone this time."

Dillon shifted, leaning toward Gracie. "Who are these people? Do you know anything about the family?"

"Not really . . . only that they're scary. No one gets in their way. I don't know exactly what they do, but I have a feeling it's not all aboveboard. One time I asked and . . ." She cringed. "Angelino backed me against a wall and pulled a knife on me."

Dillon's eyes widened.

"If I marry Constantine now, they're going to force me to sign the company over to him. Even if they make me seem crazy and incompetent, I have no doubt they will still kill me."

Dillon's throat clenched at the thought.

Suddenly, things made sense, and he felt a touch of remorse over making the woman muck the stalls.

Gracie stared at her sandwich another moment, almost like she wanted to eat it. Then she stood so quickly her chair nearly toppled behind her. "I should probably leave. Get out of your hair. Did I make enough to pay what I needed for the boat?"

"You did," Dillon said.

"Then there's no reason for me to stay." She stepped to the door. "I'm sorry for the trouble I caused."

Dillon stared at her, questions hurdling through his mind. "Where are you going to go, Gracie?"

"I have no idea. But I'll figure something out."

"He's going to find you, you know." Dillon hated to be the bearer of bad news, but Gracie had to realize that. "He's going to find a way to get you to marry him."

She shuddered. "I know. But I don't know what to do."

His mind raced. What would stop this guy from forcing Gracie to marry him? It sounded like he'd do anything to make it happen—even kill.

There was only one solution that Dillon could think of.

But the idea was crazy.

More than crazy. Maybe it was insane.

But was it the only thing that would work?

His mind raced.

Finally, he locked gazes with Gracie as he realized he had nothing to lose. "There's only one solution I can think of that would stop this guy."

Gracie's hopeful eyes searched his. "What's that?"

Dillon shrugged. "You have to marry someone else."

CHAPTER THIRTEEN

GRACIE HADN'T HEARD Dillon correctly. She *couldn't* have.

She almost wanted to laugh at how outlandish his solution was.

There were *so* many things wrong with it.

"Nice idea, but who exactly am I going to find who will marry me?" Gracie didn't bother to hide the disbelief from her voice.

"You don't have any ex-boyfriends who secretly pine after you?"

"No."

"A single friend who could be a love match?"

"No."

"A—"

"Look," Gracie interrupted. "Nice try. But there's no one. Believe me."

Dillon raised his chin, his gaze unwavering. "Then what about me?"

Her eyes widened.

She hadn't been expecting that. Not by any stretch of the imagination. Had she even heard the man correctly?

"You? Why . . . ? What . . . ?" She couldn't even find the right questions to ask.

Dillon shrugged. "It could purely be a business arrangement."

Gracie shook her head, trying to comprehend his suggestion. "A business arrangement? You're going to need to spell that out. Because people usually get married for love, at best. Or lust, at worst. We don't fall into any of the quadrants of that chart."

Dillon shifted, still unflustered at the conversation.

He was serious, wasn't he? He thought she should consider his . . . proposal.

"Look, it's like this," he started. "I have no desire to fall in love again. Ever. I tried it once, and it ended in disaster. As far as I'm concerned, my heart is closed for business. Permanently. And you—"

"I have no desire to fall in love either," Gracie

filled in, his idea making a little more sense. "I'm better off single, without complications. Anyone I marry, I'll question whether or not they have ulterior motives."

"Exactly." Dillon nodded. "Take the emotion out of it, and the arrangement makes sense."

Gracie thought about it another moment. It was true—if she married Dillon, Constantine wouldn't have any legs to stand on. There was no way he could try to force her hand. There was no way he could take over her parents' business.

But the idea was crazy.

And Dillon didn't seem like the type to jump into something like this. Not that Gracie knew the man that well. But she sensed he was the level-headed type.

"What's in it for you?" Gracie halfway dreaded hearing Dillon's answer to that question, but she braced herself for it.

There had to be something in it for him. People just didn't volunteer to do something like this on a whim or for fun.

He had to see this as mutually beneficial in some way.

"Easy," Dillon started. "My mom has been heart-broken ever since my wife left me six years ago. She worries about me constantly. Tells me I need a good woman. Tries to fix me up. Basically, she drives me insane."

"Okay . . ." That still didn't seem like a valid enough reason to go through these drastic measures.

"She's coming next week. It would make her feel so much better if she thought I'd finally found someone."

"That's the only thing you'd be getting out of this arrangement?" Gracie needed to be sure they were on the same page.

"There is one other thing . . ."

Gracie shifted as dread filled her. She *knew* it! He did have something else in mind.

"What's that?" she asked.

"When you take over your parents' business . . . I need you to run an article about the horses here on the island," he said. "A spread just ran in another publication about a possible resort being built here. We need to stop that from happening by telling people how important it is to preserve the horses' way of life here."

"It's that important to you?" Gracie questioned.

"Absolutely. These horses have been here for me when no one else has. At first, at least. Eventually, the people here in town became like family, and their land is being threatened. I'd do anything to stop it."

"Including marrying me?"

He stared at her another moment. "Including that."

Gracie's eyebrows shot up. She hadn't expected his words.

Was Dillon serious? Looking at him now, he appeared to be. He didn't seem like the type to break out with "just kidding!"

"If we do this, we need to decide soon," he said. "Constantine is already on the island looking for you."

Sweat covered her hands. "But . . . I don't believe in divorce. My parents . . . they were together twenty-four years."

"You were going to marry Constantine."

Dillon had a point. "The sacrifice seemed worth it—especially if it saved Max. With you, it's different. I don't want to ruin your life."

"Your life is the only one that deserves to be ruined?"

"At least, I have only myself to blame. If I mess up your future . . . I won't forgive myself."

"I meant it when I said I never want to fall in love again, that this is purely a business arrangement.

And, you should know, my parents were married twenty-five years before my father died. I understand exactly what you're saying."

"I'm sorry to hear that."

Dillon shifted. "Look, I'm not going to beg you. Not at all. You can make your own choices. But this guy isn't going to leave you alone until he gets what he wants. I think both of us know that."

"You would really do this for me?" Gracie stared at Dillon, hating the pressure she felt mounting inside her.

He shrugged. "Like I said, it's mutually beneficial. I want to save this island—and get my mom off my back."

"Marriage is for life," she said, feeling like the reminder was worth repeating again.

"I agree. But I'm not looking for anything. We can live our separate lives under the same roof."

"And never date anyone else again?" Gracie desperately wanted to get in this man's headspace and figure out what he was thinking.

"That's not a problem for me. In fact, I welcome the opportunity."

Now that Dillon mentioned it . . . "That's not a problem for me either. I hate dating."

He shrugged and waited for her response.

Gracie nibbled on the side of her mouth, her thoughts racing still. "What's the sleeping arrangement?"

"We can have our own rooms. We'll be . . . housemates."

She quirked an eyebrow. "Really?"

"Really." Dillon's gaze didn't waver.

Gracie thought about it another moment before extending her hand. "It's a deal."

DID DILLON really know what he was doing?

He had no idea.

But his proposal seemed like a good idea.

He'd meant his words. He had no desire to fall in love and try to find a happy ever after again.

Last time, his relationship had ended in disaster and heartbreak. Dillon wouldn't put himself in that position again.

But if Gracie was married to him . . . there was no way she could marry Constantine. A bully would be defeated. And maybe the wild horses of Cape Corral would get some of the attention they deserved.

It seemed like a win-win every way Dillon looked at it.

Besides, if the two of them were under the same roof, then Dillon could protect Gracie.

Because he had no doubt this Constantine man would try to kill her, if he had the chance.

Dillon took Gracie's outstretched hand, trying to ignore how soft her skin was as they shook on it.

"What now?" She pulled her hand back into her lap and stared at him.

"Now . . . I can call the minister and see if he'll do the ceremony."

"It's that easy, huh?" Doubt rang through her voice.

"We'll have to get the official license over at the county offices. We could do that tomorrow."

"And you said we'll have separate bedrooms, right?"

Dillon almost chuckled, but he didn't. "Yes, separate bedrooms. I'll be the perfect gentleman. I promise."

Gracie stared at him a moment, as if contemplating the truth in his words.

Finally, she nodded. "Okay. Let's do it—if you're sure. I don't want to pull you into something that you'll regret."

"I don't believe in regrets. You make decisions,

and you live with them. You learn. You go on. End of story."

"Sounds like a good philosophy." Gracie glanced at her sweatshirt. "Is this what I'm wearing for the ceremony?"

"We can work something out. Just give me a few minutes." Dillon knew just who to call to help.

CHAPTER FOURTEEN

AS GRACIE STOOD in a bedroom at the local inn and looked in the full-length mirror, her eyes widened at her reflection.

Earlier today, she'd been dressed in a designer gown. Her hair had been fixed by one of the best stylists in the DC area. Her makeup had been exquisite and perfect.

But she didn't feel as beautiful then as she did now.

Dillon's friend, a woman named Emmy Sutherland, had let Gracie borrow a white dress.

The clothing was casual, more of a sundress with strappy shoulders, a fitted bodice, and an A-line skirt. The outfit made Gracie feel somehow younger and more alive—lighter.

She'd taken a shower. But, instead of straightening her blonde hair as she normally did, she let it dry naturally in waves. Instead of slathering on makeup, she used the concealer, mascara, and lip gloss Emmy provided.

"You look gorgeous." Emmy stared at Gracie's reflection and gave an approving nod.

Emmy had been nothing but hospitable. The woman was close to Gracie's age, but, where Gracie was short with petite features, Emmy was tall with long, dark hair and an all-natural beauty. The woman's smile could light up a room, and she had a friendliness about her that made Gracie instantly trust her—and Gracie couldn't say that about many people.

"This will definitely work." Gracie ran her hand down the skirt of the dress. "Thank you."

Emmy smiled and stepped back. "Of course."

A pause stretched between them, and Gracie knew what was coming next. She braced herself for the upcoming conversation.

Emmy wouldn't be in her right mind if she didn't ask a few questions, at least.

"So . . . you and Dillon?" Emmy crossed her long, thin arms across her chest.

Gracie nodded, trying to push down her nerves.

Did she really know what she was doing right now? Would she later regret her impulsive choice?

She knew it was a possibility.

But Gracie had meant what she had said. She had no desire to fall in love or have any type of romantic entanglements. It sounded like Dillon didn't either.

Right now, all she wanted was to keep her parents' legacies alive and to stay far away from Constantine and whatever he was planning.

If she could do those things, Gracie would be a happy woman.

Besides, if she thought about this arrangement too much, she just might go running again. She knew the idea was crazy.

But her life was crazy right now. Crazy times called for crazy measures. That wasn't the saying, but still . . . it seemed to fit.

"I know it's unconventional," Gracie told Emmy. "But this is for the best."

Emmy stared at her another moment before nodding. "Dillon is a really great guy. He can be a little gruff at times, but who wouldn't be after what happened with his first wife?"

Gracie's gaze darted to Emmy, and she tried not to show her surprise—or her nerves. Dillon had mentioned their failed relationship earlier, but now Gracie was curious. "What happened with his first wife?"

Emmy's eyes widened, and she took a step back, shaking her head apologetically. "I thought you knew. Never mind."

Part of Gracie wanted to know what had happened. But another part realized that the less she knew about this man, the better.

From here on out, they would be roommates.

For life.

Gracie swallowed hard at that thought.

Was that what she was doing? Giving herself a life sentence to a loveless marriage?

The possibility should scare her more than it did.

Just as the thought went through her head, a TV in the other room caught her ear. Why did the voice coming across the airwaves sound familiar?

Almost as if in a trance, Gracie stepped from the bedroom where she'd been getting ready, her eyes fastened on the TV screen in the next room.

Constantine was on the news, talking to reporters. Giving a press conference, it appeared.

The camera had always loved the man with his refined features and finessed way of doing things.

His blond hair looked perfectly coiffed, as normal, but his eyes were what caught Gracie's attention. They were red-rimmed, as if he'd been crying.

Right now, he used his charisma to implore viewers.

"I believe that my fiancée, Gracie Loveland, was abducted in the moments prior to our wedding ceremony," he told the camera. "I'm offering a ten thousand-dollar reward to anyone who comes forward with information about her disappearance or her whereabouts."

Nausea gurgled in Gracie's stomach.

Constantine stared right into the screen. "Gracie, if you're out there and you can see this, know that I love you and that I'm never going to give up in my quest to find you again. Never."

As she felt her knees buckling, Gracie caught herself on the doorframe.

To anybody else, that would have sounded like a doting promise to find the love of his life.

To Gracie, she knew it was a threat.

DILLON PAUSED as he stood in the room behind the sanctuary at the Cape Corral Community

Church. A storm had whipped up outside, coming from nowhere. The showers had held off, but thunder and lightning put on a show across the horizon.

As long as it didn't rain, they'd be okay . . . right? Not that Dillon was superstitious. But rain on your wedding day? Wasn't that supposed to be the ultimate sign of bad luck?

As Dillon stood there, his thoughts went back to his first marriage.

His marriage to Lauren.

The wedding hadn't been anything like this one. Lauren's parents had probably spent twenty thousand to make the day special. No expense had been spared—including swans outside at the reception.

All that for a marriage that lasted two years.

All it had taken was one military deployment, and Lauren had realized that she wasn't cut out for that lifestyle.

Dillon wanted to say that he didn't regret their time together, but in some ways he did. Having a spouse walk out on you changed a person's outlook. Dillon knew he never wanted to put himself in a position to have his heart crushed again.

His friend Grant stepped into the room and studied him a moment. "So, you're really going to do this? No cold feet? No realization that this just might be tomfoolery at the highest level?"

Dillon tugged the sleeve of his white button-up shirt. He wore his customary jeans and cowboy boots. The white shirt clearly stated he was dressed up. In his mind, at least.

"I'm ready for this," he assured his friend.

Grant studied him for a minute. "Am I correct in assuming you've only known this woman for less than twenty-four hours?"

"Yep."

"And she was the one you rescued from the stolen boat today?"

"Yep."

"And she was also the one that was mucking the stalls earlier?"

"Another yep."

Grant shook his head and let out a skeptical chuckle. "I have no idea what is going through your head right now. But I hope you're not making a mistake, my friend."

"I don't believe in mistakes. I only believe in new opportunities to learn."

"Well, if you're wrong on this one, then you're going to have a lifetime of learning."

Dillon couldn't fault his friend for asking the

questions or giving the advice. What kind of friend would he be if he didn't?

But Dillon's decision had been made.

He was going to marry Gracie Loveland.

And marrying her would ensure that he never made the same mistakes he'd made with Lauren.

Just then, Pastor Brian Daniels stepped into the room. The man and his wife had only moved to the island a few months ago, but the couple already seemed to fit in.

"Are you ready?" Brian asked. "The bride has arrived."

Dillon nodded, pushing down a sudden swell of nerves. "Let's do this."

He stepped into the sanctuary, knowing hardly anyone would be here. He hadn't invited anybody else.

Brian would do the ceremony. Grant would be a witness, along with Emmy. Heidi—Brian's wife— would play the piano.

There was no need for a lot of fanfare.

As Dillon took his place on the stage, he glanced at the back of the church.

The doors to the sanctuary opened, and Heidi began playing the "Wedding March."

Gracie stepped inside.

Dillon sucked in a breath.

She looked . . . beautiful.

Then again, Dillon already knew the woman was gorgeous. That had never been in doubt.

But Gracie was cleaned up now. All the muck from the Currituck Sound and the hay from the stables was gone. She wasn't wearing a tattered wedding dress or oversized jeans.

Instead, the dress that Emmy had let her borrow fit Gracie in all the right places.

As soon as the thought went through Dillon's head, he wondered for the first time if maybe this was a mistake.

Because it was one thing to marry someone he wasn't attracted to.

And it was a totally different story to marry someone who took his breath away.

CHAPTER FIFTEEN

GRACIE COULDN'T GET Constantine's words out of her mind as she slowly walked down the aisle.

I'll never stop looking for you. Never.

Her throat tightened until she could hardly breathe.

What was she doing? The answer was a little too clear: she was dragging Dillon into this whole mess. What if he became a casualty of this situation?

Please, Lord. No . . .

She glanced up at the front of the church as she gripped the wildflower bouquet Emmy had handed her. When she saw Dillon's broad, imposing figure standing beside the minister, she sucked in a breath.

Goodness gracious, the man was handsome.

He was definitely the kind of man who could

take care of himself—and who would take care of her.

That didn't stop the deluge of guilt from filling her.

Instead of focusing on it, Gracie soaked Dillon in for another moment.

She was marrying a cowboy.

A *cowboy*.

How was this city girl doing such a one-eighty? This wasn't anything she'd ever seen herself doing.

Gracie had never even thought of herself as one to have a crush on someone who'd stepped out of a Western. But, as she looked at Dillon now, how could she not? That white shirt with those jeans and cowboy boots . . . he formed quite the picture.

Her throat went dry.

Maybe this was a terrible idea. The two of them were both jumping into something that would consume them for the rest of their lives.

Yet another part of Gracie didn't want to back out now.

Marrying Dillon was the only thing that would ensure she could never marry Constantine.

And if that was the case, then Constantine could never gain control of her parents' company.

Gracie knew the logic might be twisted, but she

was also realistic—at least, she *could* be realistic—when it counted.

Nothing had ever counted more than this moment right now.

She climbed the steps to the stage of the traditional-looking church building with its dark wooden pews and arched windows. A baptistry with beautiful stained glass featuring a picture of a dove ascending into heaven stretched behind them.

A dove . . . it represented hope and a promise.

Just like she was making a promise to Dillon before God right now.

Gracie looked away from the image and turned to face her future groom.

Something in his gaze had changed also.

Was he surprised to see her dressed like this?

Or maybe he was having second thoughts too.

Gracie swallowed hard, wondering what the outcome of this evening would be.

Had she chosen to protect herself physically while dying a slow emotional death?

She didn't know the answer to that question.

DILLON BARELY HEARD what the pastor was saying.

But he could hardly take his eyes off Gracie.

He hadn't expected to feel the rush of attraction that he did for her.

Why should he? She was infuriating. Feisty. Headstrong.

None of the qualities he'd ever looked for in a woman before.

But if Dillon were honest with himself, he'd admit that another part of him was intrigued.

"Dillon McGrath, do you take this woman to be your lawfully wedded wife?"

He looked at Gracie, at her green eyes as they implored him.

Implored him?

Yet that's exactly what she seemed to be doing.

He swallowed hard. "I do."

"Gracie Loveland, do you take this man to be your lawfully wedded husband?"

She hesitated just a moment.

Long enough for Dillon to hold his breath.

Was she going to say no?

Finally, she nodded. "I do."

Just as she said the words, thunder clapped

outside. The sound was so loud that everyone in the building seemed to jump.

Was that God disapproving of what they'd done?

Dillon sure hoped it wasn't.

"You may kiss your bride," Brian announced.

Dillon stared at Gracie, unsure how to proceed.

How had he not thought this through? He'd promised two separate bedrooms. But a kiss to seal their marriage?

It hadn't been discussed.

As the pastor's words rang in the air, Dillon realized that everybody was watching and waiting.

No one in this room was under the illusion that he or Gracie were doing this for love.

But he didn't want to make a spectacle of them either.

Instead, Dillon stepped closer, his gaze glowing down at Gracie.

She didn't step back as he'd expected. Instead, the woman—his bride—stared up at him, surprising stubbornness in her gaze.

Her thoughts mirrored his own, didn't they?

She knew this was crazy. Yet she was desperate.

Just like Dillon.

He leaned closer, hesitating only a moment before brushing his lips against hers.

The zing of electricity he felt as he did sent him scurrying back more quickly than he'd planned.

That couldn't have been right. There was no way he'd felt any electricity with this woman.

It was just the stress of today. His lack of sleep. *Anything* but attraction.

Gracie's gaze quickly fluttered away from his as their two witnesses applauded.

But the sound was nearly lost.

There was really nothing to applaud for. This whole ceremony and marriage were simply for convenience's sake and nothing more.

Dillon turned toward his friends. "Thank you for coming. I really appreciate it, especially since it was last minute."

Who said marriage couldn't be practical? Why did it have to be warm, fuzzy feelings and dreams of being happy forever?

Dillon had done the right thing.

No regrets.

As long as his heart didn't get involved, that should be easy enough.

Grant clamped his hand down on Dillon's shoulder. "Well, as my grandma would say, blow up my dress and call me pretty. What can I say except congratulations, man. I wish the best for both of you."

Strangely enough, his friend almost sounded sincere.

With a wave to everyone, Dillon took Gracie's hand in his. The act was just for show. Dillon knew he'd let go as soon as they were out of sight from anybody.

As they stepped through the front door of the church, lightning lit the area around them.

Gracie gasped beside him.

When Dillon followed her gaze, he saw a lone figure standing on a sand dune in the distance.

Whoever it was, the man was watching them.

Was it Constantine?

There was only one way to find out.

Dillon took off in a run after the man.

CHAPTER SIXTEEN

"WHAT'S GOING ON?" Emmy appeared beside Gracie, her eyes narrowed in curiosity.

"There was a man over there." Gracie couldn't stop the tremble from controlling her voice. "He was watching us, and Dillon went after him."

As soon as Grant heard what she said, he took off in a run also.

Emmy pulled Gracie back into the church building and out of the stormy weather. "We're better off in here."

"I guess we are."

"Those guys are good at what they do," Emmy assured her. "They'll be fine."

"I hope so."

After a few moments of silence, Emmy cleared her throat.

"So . . ." Emmy rocked back on her heels. "Congratulations." Emmy's statement sounded more like a question.

"Thanks." But Gracie's words were lackluster.

Maybe reality hadn't sunk in yet.

But for just a brief moment, when Dillon had kissed her, all her problems had disappeared.

Gracie still wasn't sure where these thoughts and feelings were coming from. But when she'd experienced Dillon's lips brushing against hers, something had jolted inside her.

It made no sense.

Even when she and Constantine had been dating, she'd never felt a jarring spark like that.

She'd dated a few other people before Constantine, but she'd never felt that connection that she had so desperately longed for. That only led her to one conclusion—that storybook romances simply didn't exist.

Why did Gracie suddenly wonder if her mind could change?

It was a question for another time.

Right now, Gracie pulled her arms over her chest and waited.

She hoped that Dillon was okay.

Because if the man who'd been out there was Constantine . . . she shuddered at the thought. At one time, Gracie would have thought that the man was simply an astute businessman. But now it was becoming more and more clear he was a vile criminal.

She'd never forgive herself if he did something to Dillon.

Despite the cowboy's unyielding personality, he'd done nothing more than look out for her. And that was something she was grateful for.

Please, Lord. Protect him.

And please help today not to be the biggest mistake of my life.

AS SOON AS Dillon got close to the man, he propelled himself through the air. His hands caught the stranger's legs, and he tackled him to the ground.

The man struggled to get away, but Dillon pinned his arms to the sandy dune beneath them.

As lightning flashed in the sky again, Dillon squinted.

This man wasn't Constantine.

Dillon had never seen this man before. Someone with a smaller build, wire-framed glasses, and curly, light-brown hair.

"Who are you?" As the question left Dillon's lips, Grant appeared beside him and glowered down at the man.

"Can I at least stand up?"

Grant gave Dillon a nod. As Dillon released the man he had pinned on the ground, Grant grabbed the man's arm and jerked him to his feet. They hovered on either side of the stranger, daring the man to run away.

The man rolled his shoulders back, as if annoyed by this confrontation. "Who I am is none of your business."

"I'd say it is," Grant said. "What were you doing watching us tonight?"

"Is that a crime?"

"Voyeurism? I'd say it is." Dillon's jaw hardened. "Now, do you want to do things the easy way or the hard way?"

"You guys are just blowing smoke." The man brushed sand off his shoulders. "But if you must know, I'm studying the island and trying to understand the dynamics here."

"Why are you doing that?" Grant asked.

The man reached for a pocket at the front of his shirt, silently asking for permission. When Grant nodded, he pulled a card out. "My name is PJ Anderson. I work for the Fergusons."

As soon as Dillon heard the name *Ferguson*, he knew this man was going to be trouble—just a different kind of trouble than he'd originally assumed.

"Why were you watching us?" Dillon demanded.

"The family hired me to try to be a negotiator between them and the islanders. As you know, they plan to build a resort on the north tip of the island. I understand that locals are against this, and we want to work together to find a solution that will make everyone happy."

"So they brought you in?" Dillon shook his head, watching as more lightning flashed offshore. "Locals won't change their minds."

"It's amazing how a little bit of incentive is all it takes for some people to change their minds." PJ smiled, the action a little too smug.

Dillon stepped closer, already irritated with the man. "Just what are the Fergusons planning?"

He couldn't even begin to fathom what the corrupt family might be thinking. Dillon knew one thing for sure—the family was shrewd. They'd do whatever necessary to get what they wanted.

PJ shrugged. "We're considering all our options."

"If you're doing anything illegal, we're going to find out about it," Grant said.

"I would never be a proponent of doing something illegal." But the haughty look on PJ's face said otherwise.

Dillon's finger darted toward the man. "If I ever catch you watching me again, there will be consequences."

"That's good to know," PJ called as he took a step back. "Don't think I won't press charges if you ever handle me like that again. If the press happened to find out about an altercation that I had with the local fire chief, I'm sure they'd have a field day with it."

Anger burned through Dillon's blood. This man had done his research. He knew exactly who Dillon was.

Instead of responding, Dillon remained quiet.

He knew if he spoke, he'd regret it.

Dillon would deal with this man later.

For now, he needed to deal with his new bride.

CHAPTER SEVENTEEN

I WILL FIND YOU.

I'm on your tail.

In fact, I'm only a few steps away.

He fought a smile at the realization.

Plastering on a polite expression, he knocked at the cottage door. The place was located on the edge of the Currituck Sound and was a true waterman's home, complete with a dock and a whole wall of crab traps. The scent of the sea rose around him—fish, crabs, salt.

But he cared about none of those things.

A moment later, a man with a long, gray beard answered.

Mr. Dunleavy.

"Can I help you?" Dunleavy scratched his head as if confused by the late-night visitor.

He'd expected that reaction, especially considering the time and the fact that it was storming outside.

He pulled his raincoat farther over his head, trying to make it appear like he was trying to stay dry. In reality, he needed to conceal his features.

"I'm sorry to bother you at this time of night, but I have a question for you," he started. "Someone at the gas station down the road told me that your boat was stolen this morning."

The man nodded, but only kept the door cracked open a few inches. "That's right. But the police found it. If that's what you're here about, then everything's taken care of."

He reached forward, not ready to end this conversation with this man yet. "I was wondering if they apprehended the person responsible."

The man, Mr. Dunleavy, shrugged. "It's been taken care of. Restitution has been paid. Everything's just fine."

Dunleavy started to shut the door again.

"Do you mind me asking who took it?" he asked. "Who stole your boat?"

The man almost seemed to bristle. "Why does it matter?"

"Someone I care about is missing. I believe she might have come this way, and I'm wondering if she's the person who stole your boat."

The man stared at him, as if processing what he said.

"To be truthful, I didn't get this person's name," Dunleavy finally said. "But it was a woman, and she seemed very apologetic and very sweet."

Interesting. That could definitely fit Gracie.

"You said she paid you back?" he repeated. "But you didn't see her?"

"A check is coming," the man said. "I'm the old-fashioned type who prefers to trust people. What can I say?"

"You don't know any other details?"

"That's correct." The man shifted. "I wish I could help you more, but I can't. Now if you don't mind, I would really like to get to bed. I'm a fisherman, and my day starts early."

He nodded. "You have been very helpful. Thank you."

"I hope you find your friend."

"I do too."

Now he had a better idea about where he needed to look.

He was going to go back to Cape Corral.

Because he felt confident that that was where he would find Gracie.

And when he did . . . she would pay.

CHAPTER EIGHTEEN

GRACIE NOTICED that Dillon was quiet on the ride to his place.

He'd briefly explained to her what had happened on the sand dune. But he didn't seem in the mood to offer many details.

That was just as well with her. Gracie didn't mind the quiet—except for the fact that her thoughts were churning.

Several minutes later, Dillon pulled his truck in front of a cottage. Some of the homes here on the island were built high up on stilts. But not this one.

The house had been painted yellow—at least, that's how it looked in the glow of Dillon's headlights. A screened porch stretched across the front of the building, and woods lined the backside.

It looked cozy enough.

"Welcome home," Dillon said, an almost dry amusement to his voice.

Gracie's throat tightened at his words.

Home.

It was so hard to hear that word associated with a place she'd never been.

But she knew this moment was coming when she'd agreed to all this.

She pressed her eyes shut and prayed she hadn't made the biggest mistake of her life.

A moment later, Dillon appeared at her side of the truck and helped her out. They walked together toward the front door, her anxiety building with every step.

Gracie was supposed to be on her way to Aruba right now. On her honeymoon. With Constantine.

When she looked at things in that light, then the situation she was actually in right now didn't seem as bad. She'd dodged that bullet, so to speak.

Dillon opened the door and started inside.

Gracie remained on the porch. "You're not going to carry me across the threshold?"

She was partly egging Dillon on. Aggravating him distracted her from her problems.

She hoped that wasn't a problem.

Dillon stared at her a moment, some of the irritation in his eyes turning to humor. "Is that really what you want me to do?"

"You have to throw me some kind of bone right now."

Dillon stared at her, his eyes brooding and . . . something else. After a couple of seconds, he finally leaned forward and scooped her into his arms.

Gracie had been trying to be funny, to break the awkward moment.

But as she felt his strong arms beneath her, she inadvertently trembled.

She hadn't expected to have this reaction to the man—again. First when he kissed her at the wedding ceremony, and now when he'd lifted her into his arms.

But the feeling would pass. Gracie was sure of it.

He nudged the door open and carried her inside the warm house that smelled faintly of leather. Gently, he set her on the oak-stained floor.

"Hope you like it," Dillon murmured.

She cleared her throat, straightening her dress as she tried to gather her thoughts.

Instead of focusing on her pounding heart, Gracie surveyed the space.

For a bachelor pad, the home wasn't bad. The

decorations could use a few feminine touches. Maybe some greenery and throw pillows. A few pictures.

But Gracie could work with this cottage.

Dillon took her elbow. "I'll show you to your room."

His touch burned into her, but she didn't pull away. She hardly had a chance. The man whisked her from the door.

The whole place was only one story. Dillon led her through the living room and kitchen into the hallway that stretched beyond that. He passed by the first two doors before opening a door at the end of the hallway.

"I hope this will work for you," he said.

Gracie glanced at the simple space with its metal framed bed and white bedspread. "It will be fine. I know I seem high-maintenance, but I'm not."

Dillon said nothing. In the silence, Gracie wondered exactly what this man thought of her. Maybe he didn't think high-maintenance—maybe he thought she was simply high-strung.

It didn't matter either way. Gracie had made her choice, and now she was going to live with it.

So was Dillon.

DILLON LAY IN BED, darkness and silence surrounding him.

Yet he couldn't sleep.

Was it the weight of what he'd done today that kept him awake? Or the fact that Gracie Loveland was sleeping in the room across the hall?

No, not Gracie Loveland. Gracie *McGrath*.

Tomorrow, the two of them would need to go to the county court building to get their official marriage license.

Had he really just gotten married again? The thought seemed surreal. It would take time for this to sink in.

Before the two of them had said good night, Gracie had told him about the press briefing Constantine had given earlier.

Dillon's muscles had tensed with each new detail she revealed.

Afterward, he'd checked all the doors and windows at his cottage at least twice. Dillon also placed his gun on the nightstand beside him, so he'd be ready to act if it came down to it.

But he hoped it didn't come down to that.

Dillon hoped that this guy left Gracie alone.

But he had a feeling that wouldn't happen.

He turned over in bed, still determined to get some sleep. But details continued to repeat in his mind. Rescuing Gracie today. Marrying her. Feeling how soft her lips felt against his.

That last one was something that he surely needed to forget about.

But that was going to be easier said than done.

After trying, for what felt like hours, to unsuccessfully fall sleep, Dillon finally grabbed the laptop from his nightstand and opened it. Out of curiosity, he Googled "Gracie Loveland."

Pages and pages popped up.

The woman was a natural when it came to social media.

He scrolled through the pictures. In each one, Gracie's face practically glowed. Her smile made it hard to look away.

Except in more recent photos.

As Dillon scrolled closer to the date of her wedding, he noticed the light had disappeared from Gracie's gaze.

Being with Constantine had broken her, hadn't it? The ordeal would be a lot for anyone to go through.

There were also articles about her parents' tragic

death in the car accident. Mentions of how Gracie would receive their media conglomerate when she turned thirty.

There were a lot of reasons someone might want to take control of a company like that. Not only for the money it probably brought in. Controlling what kind of information was being released could be powerful.

So what was this Constantine guy after? Money? Power? Or both?

A new article caught Dillon's eye.

Gracie's house up in DC had burned down earlier today. His eyes narrowed as he kept reading.

The police suspected that Gracie may have set her own home on fire. A neighbor saw her there earlier that afternoon.

Which wasn't possible.

Because she'd been with Dillon.

Realization dawned on him.

Someone was setting her up.

Trying to paint her as unstable.

This person was going to extremes to do so.

The only thing Dillon found comfort in was knowing that he could keep Gracie safe . . . for as long as she let him.

CHAPTER NINETEEN

GRACIE DIDN'T KNOW what to expect when she awoke the next morning.

Quite frankly, she was surprised she'd been able to sleep at all. Perhaps yesterday's events had left her exhausted. It was the only thing that might explain her ability to rest in the middle of this turmoil.

As the sun rose outside, she stared up at the ceiling, part of her not wanting to get out of bed. When she did get up, she would be facing a life that looked a lot different.

She was married.

She had really done it.

She'd tied the knot with . . . not Constantine but *Dillon*.

Her marriage still seemed surreal.

There was no undoing what had been done. Now she needed to make the best of it. That didn't mean there wasn't part of her that wanted to live in denial for a little bit longer.

Finally, Gracie threw the covers off so she could get dressed for the day. Thankfully, Emmy had loaned her a few things to wear until Gracie could buy her own clothes. The woman had muttered some kind of joke about opening up a boutique on the island, and Gracie had the impression this wasn't the first time Emmy had helped clothe someone.

As soon as Gracie could get to her money, she'd pay Emmy back. Gracie had never been one for handouts. She preferred standing on her own two feet.

She gathered the clothes and toiletries she needed and cracked her door open. She looked up and down the hallway but saw no one.

Clutching her clothes to her chest, she tiptoed into the bathroom.

Once inside, she locked the door behind her—just to be safe.

As she turned around, she glanced out the window.

She sucked in a breath at what she saw.

A truck drove past Dillon's house.

She could barely make out the figure inside.

But it almost looked like . . . Constantine.

The man drove slowly, as if scouting out the area.

But he didn't stop near Dillon's place.

Was that because he didn't know Gracie was here?

She could only hope that was the case.

But even if it was . . . how long would she be able to remain hidden?

Because there was one thing she knew for sure—Constantine was not going to give up.

―――――――

DILLON HAD DECIDED to take the morning off work. He was drinking his black coffee and reading the newspaper when he heard footsteps down the hallway.

Gracie must be awake.

He folded the paper and stood. Neither of them had eaten very much yesterday. With that thought in mind, he pulled out the items to make some biscuits and gravy. It was his mom's recipe, and the dish was still one of his favorites.

But he paused halfway through cooking.

What if Gracie didn't eat gluten? Or meat? Or pork?

There was so much he didn't know about her.

Actually, Dillon hardly knew *anything* about the woman.

If he thought about that too much, he'd realize that fact was unnerving.

So it was best if he didn't think about it.

Just as Dillon pulled the biscuits from the oven, he looked up and saw Gracie standing in the entrance of the kitchen. The sleeves of her pink shirt were pulled over her hands and she wore some black leggings with fuzzy socks.

Dillon sucked in a breath at the sight of her.

The woman shouldn't look that good wearing an outfit like that.

But she did.

That realization meant only one thing—Dillon was in some serious trouble.

"Good morning." Dillon's words sounded scratchier than he'd intended.

"Good morning." Gracie surveyed the kitchen. "Is there anything I can do to help?"

"Actually, I'm just finishing this up. If you'd like to have a seat, I'll bring you some breakfast."

Her eyebrows shot into the air. "Can I expect this every morning?"

He let out a chuckle. "I wouldn't, if I were you. I usually make some breakfast burritos at the beginning of the week and then heat them up every morning. It's . . . practical."

"It sounds like it." Gracie offered an almost shy smile as she sat down.

Dillon grabbed a mug from the cabinet.

"How do you take your coffee?" It seemed weird to ask someone he'd just married that question. But nothing about this situation was normal.

"Two sugars and a little cream."

"Coming up."

He fixed the drink just as Gracie requested before setting it on the table in front of her. He then grabbed their food and sat across from her.

It was their first morning as husband and wife.

And it couldn't feel more awkward.

He needed to tell her about the fact that her house had burned down. He decided to let her eat first.

"I have a little good news," he started.

"What's that? I could use some good news."

"We found your wallet in the boat. I'm afraid

your purse or car keys or whatever else you had with you is gone. But at least you have your ID now."

"That is good news, especially if we're going to get a marriage license, right?"

"The timing couldn't have been better."

Gracie held her coffee mug in the air and cleared her throat. "There's something you should know."

Did she already know about the fire? She didn't appear to have a cell phone or computer. How would she have found out?

"What's going on?" Dillon asked.

"I glanced out the window this morning . . . and I thought I saw Constantine."

Dillon's muscles bristled. He hadn't expected to hear that. "What do you mean?"

"I mean . . . I can't be sure. But a truck drove by. The man inside . . . he looked like Constantine."

"Was he looking at my house, in particular?"

"It's hard to say," Gracie said. "To me, it looked like he was searching for something. But he didn't slow in front of your place as if he was staking it out or anything."

"How certain are you that it was him?"

Gracie rubbed the side of her coffee mug. "I'm not certain at all. But we already know he was on the island. If he has any suspicion that I'm here, he's not going to stop looking."

Dillon didn't like the sound of that. He leaned back. "Tell me more about him. What does he do for a living?"

"His family owns a business. They sell pillows." She shrugged.

"Pillows?"

"Yep, pillows. The kind you sleep on. Memory foam, cotton, hybrid."

"What did Constantine do for the family business?"

Gracie took another sip of coffee before saying, "I always wondered that. He didn't seem to do much, but he always had money."

"I'm going to talk to people on the island today. See if anyone gave him a boat ride over from the mainland or if he's rented one of the houses here."

She nodded. "That sounds good."

"I watched the video he released last night," Dillon continued. "I was trying to determine where it was taken. I couldn't tell. The building behind him was pretty nondescript. I listened for environmental noises—seagulls or the ocean. I didn't hear anything."

"So you don't know if he made the video here or somewhere else?"

"I figure he didn't make it here," Dillon said. "I would have noticed the reporters on the island. I just wanted to know if he was close. We'll keep looking into it."

"Thank you," Gracie said.

"One more thing . . ."

"What's that?"

Dillon told her about her house burning down.

CHAPTER TWENTY

GRACIE PULLED her ball cap lower and made sure her sunglasses were in place as she stepped off the boat. The disguise wasn't brilliant, but at least it concealed most of her face. That, when combined with the leggings and oversized tunic she wore, should make her unrecognizable.

She hoped.

"You look a little green," Dillon muttered as he released her hand and she wobbled on the dock.

He stood close enough to catch her if necessary.

She scowled. She knew she shouldn't. Knew it wasn't Dillon's fault.

But she scowled anyway. "Boats and I don't go together, apparently."

Was Dillon trying not to smile? Did this amuse him?

That only made her grumpiness more pungent. Ever since she heard her house had burned down, she'd been in a mood.

It was the house she'd been raised in by her parents.

"At least you didn't throw up," Dillon offered.

"It's not too late. And, if I do, I know where to aim."

Dillon chuckled as he led her to a car he left on this side of the water. They had to drive to the county offices for the marriage certificate. "Someone is *not* in a good mood. I suppose this isn't the honeymoon you dreamed about?"

She wished she had something to throw at him, but she didn't.

She and Dillon had traveled across the Currituck Sound to the mainland. The hum of the boat engine had made it nearly impossible to talk—and Gracie hadn't complained. The quiet had been nice—especially quiet from conversations like this.

Despite that, she'd been counting the minutes until they reached dry land.

She tugged at her hat again as they started down the road. Because of Constantine's media blitz last night, Gracie needed to lie low for a while. If someone recognized her, they'd call the police.

They might assume that Dillon had abducted her, and that was the last thing Gracie wanted. Well, maybe it was tempting—but only because the man was infuriating at times.

She simply needed to disappear until these things passed, she reminded herself.

If they passed.

They pulled up to the Circuit Court Building entirely too quickly.

A rumble of nerves rushed through Gracie as she stepped out of the car.

"You ready to do this?" Dillon turned toward her, a surprising measure of sincerity in his gaze as he asked the question. His earlier glibness was gone.

"I'm not going to try to run off a cliff again, if that's what you're asking."

"Good to know."

A sick feeling swirled in Gracie's stomach, but she tried to ignore it.

She and Dillon had said their vows before God. Now they needed to follow through to make it legal.

Second-guessing herself would do no good now.

As they went inside, Gracie's hand went to her stomach. Her seasickness still wasn't completely gone—that's what she would blame her queasiness on, at least. She crossed her arms over her chest, giving Dillon one last dirty look as he accidentally nudged her.

She had to break out of this funk and soon.

They walked to the front desk to sign in.

The woman behind the desk stared at them as she smacked her gum and twirled a piece of her dark hair. "You two here to file a complaint?"

"A complaint?" Gracie felt a knot of confusion form between her eyes. Then she cleared her throat, pulling herself together. "No, we're here to get a marriage license."

The woman's eyes wavered back and forth from Dillon then back to Gracie. Then she burst into a nasal chuckle that turned into full out laughter.

"The two of you? A marriage license?" She laughed a few more moments before wiping the tears beneath her eyes. "I'm sorry. I don't know what got into me."

They waited for her to calm down.

"That just makes my day." Finally, she grabbed a clipboard. "Start by filling this out."

But as they went to find a seat, another round of laughter filled the air, almost as if the woman couldn't control herself.

Gracie and Dillon exchanged a glance.

Apparently, it was obvious to anyone around that the two of them were mismatched.

Was that what God thought also?

Gracie's throat clenched at the thought.

Before she could force out any more conversation, Dillon's phone rang. He muttered a few things into it, each new word causing tension to float through the air.

As soon as he ended the call, he turned to Gracie. "You should know that someone broke into the Community Safety building last night."

That hadn't been what she'd expected to hear. "I'm sorry to hear that. Was anything vandalized or stolen?"

"Only one thing." Dillon's gaze locked on Gracie's. "Your wedding dress."

———

DILLON HATED the tension that mounted inside him as he and Gracie left the county building. But it was done. The marriage license had been given to them.

With the way things had gone so far, this was going to be a long day.

Then again, he'd signed up to be together for a lifetime.

What had he been thinking?

Despite his doubts, there was one more thing he needed to do.

As they climbed back into Dillon's car, he turned to Gracie. Her face still looked pale—it had ever since the receptionist had laughed at the idea of the two of them getting married.

"I want you to wear this." Dillon slid something onto her finger.

A gold wedding band.

Gracie's eyes widened when she looked down at it. "Dillon . . . this is really beautiful."

"I think so too. It used to be my grandmother's. I would have brought it to the ceremony yesterday, but I didn't have the chance to grab it in time."

She continued to stare at the band. "You didn't have to do this."

"I know. But I wanted to. We don't know each other that well, but I want you to know that I take this seriously."

She glanced up at him, questions in her gaze— and maybe another emotion as well. "Thank you for trusting me with it."

"Of course. I can't have my wife walking

around looking like she's unattached." He offered a quick smile. "It's bad enough that she looks like she's going to throw up when she's around me."

Gracie let out a chuckle and punched his arm. "I was seasick."

"The lady at the front desk thought it was hysterical."

Gracie frowned, glancing at the ring and then at Dillon. "Do we really look miserable together?"

He leaned closer until Gracie's eyes widened at his nearness. He lowered his voice as he said, "I wouldn't worry about it."

"Why's that?" Her voice sounded thin as she asked the question.

"Because we have a whole lifetime to make each other miserable."

She broke from her daze and rolled her eyes. "Very funny."

Dillon smiled and cranked the engine. "What do you say we stop by the store and pick up a few things for you before we head back?"

"I think that sounds great."

It wasn't until they were heading down the road that Gracie mentioned the stolen wedding dress again.

"Constantine knows I'm on Cape Corral, doesn't he?" Her voice cracked.

"It's hard to say." Dillon instantly sobered. "But it's a good guess."

"What am I going to do?" A shiver raked through her body.

Dillon started to squeeze her arm but settled for patting her knee instead. "I'll make sure you're safe."

"You don't understand," Gracie rushed, fanning her face. "You don't know what kind of person he is. He doesn't care who gets in his way."

He had to stop Gracie's train of thought before she totally derailed. "It's going to be okay."

She looked up at him, moisture glimmering in her eyes. "Nothing feels okay. Nothing at all. Max betrayed me. My house burned down. My wedding dress was stolen."

Dillon's heart thumped in his chest.

Was she referring to their marriage also? If so, he couldn't blame her.

But Dillon would work hard to prove that this decision wasn't a mistake.

Maybe they would never have the romance that some marriages did. But that didn't mean they couldn't have a pleasant life together.

He hoped.

"I know I've been cranky with you this morning, but thank you for everything." She looked at him almost shyly.

It was enough to turn Dillon's bones into gelatin.

"No problem." He cleared his throat. "Now, how about we go shopping and then get back before anyone sees us?"

CHAPTER TWENTY-ONE

GRACIE FILLED her basket with several necessities at a nearby department store. As she shopped, she kept her hat pulled low and her sunglasses pushed down to the tip of her nose so she could see over the top of them.

She couldn't risk anybody recognizing her.

Dillon stayed dutifully by her side the entire time, keeping a lookout for any signs of trouble. Gracie couldn't help but feel like they were being watched, but she knew the feeling was mostly borne out of paranoia.

Her face had been plastered on the news. People would be looking for her.

Even worse—*Constantine* would be looking for her.

Gracie didn't want to take any chances—yet she couldn't avoid picking up a few things to get her through until this passed. *If* it passed.

No, she couldn't think like that.

There had to be an end in sight . . . right?

Finally, when Gracie had grabbed everything she needed, she looked up at Dillon. "We can check out."

He glanced around before leading her to the register. As she put her things on the counter, guilt flooded her as Dillon pulled out his wallet to pay.

She wished she could stand on her own two feet.

But that wasn't possible right now. If she used her credit card, it could be tracked.

"I'll keep mucking the stalls for you, if that makes it better," she whispered.

Dillon let out a little chuckle and shook his head. But, as he did, he glanced around again—just as he'd been doing all day.

He wasn't taking any chances either, was he?

"That's not necessary," he murmured. "Now, come on. Let's pay so we can get back."

They quickly checked out, and, with four bags in hand, stepped toward the exit. A bright, sunny day waited for them on the other side of the doors, and it seemed like safety was in sight.

As they walked toward Dillon's truck, a woman headed into the store stopped and called to them. "Excuse me!"

Slowly, Gracie turned. As soon as she saw the woman's expression, she knew this wasn't going to be good.

"Aren't you Gracie Loveland?" The woman's eyes shot to Dillon, and she frowned.

The woman reached into her purse, probably about to grab her phone and call the police—to report that Gracie had been found.

Panic rushed through Gracie.

What was she going to do?

She hadn't come this far for things to end like this.

———

DILLON TENSED as he waited to see what would happen next.

He froze as Gracie wrapped her arm around his waist and pressed herself into him.

"I don't know who Gracie Loveland is," Gracie crooned. "But it's not me."

The woman looked up at Dillon again, her eyes still narrow, before looking back at Gracie. "You're not the woman who disappeared right before her wedding?"

"No, I don't know who that might be." Gracie squeezed him tighter. "But I'm happily married to this guy. Right, honey?"

Dillon wrapped his arm around her and kissed the top of her head. "Couldn't be happier."

As the woman stared at them another moment, Dillon held his breath, waiting to see what she would say. Had she bought Gracie's story?

Finally, a smile cracked her face. "You two are so cute. I suppose you just have some of the same features as this other woman. I'm sorry to have stopped you. I do believe people should watch out for each other, though."

"No, it's okay. Whoever this woman is that you're looking for, it sounds serious."

"Disappearing right before your wedding ceremony?" The woman shook her head and let out a long breath. "I can't even imagine. This has *Dateline Special* written all over it."

Gracie frowned. "That does sound horrible. I hope the police are able to find her."

"Me too." With those final words, the woman disappeared into the store.

As soon as she was out of sight, Gracie released her arm from around him.

Dillon instantly missed her closeness. Or maybe it was the surprise of the moment that played with his emotions.

Either way, he dared not say anything until they were back in his car.

"Quick thinking back there," he told her.

"Sorry that I had to . . . touch you. I didn't know what else to do."

"Don't feel like you have to apologize for touching me."

"It's just weird." She shrugged. "You know?"

"It is. But you covered your tracks. You did good."

"At least I did something right," she murmured.

Dillon had to wonder what that meant. Instead of asking, he cranked the engine and headed back to the boat.

CHAPTER TWENTY-TWO

WHEN THEY ARRIVED BACK at Cape Corral, Dillon asked Gracie to go into the office with him. That was fine by her.

All day, every time she'd seen any type of movement, Gracie had turned, expecting to see Constantine standing there.

She wasn't sure how much longer she could live in this state of fear.

Constantine was the only person she could think of who would have stolen her wedding dress.

And that would mean he could be here on this island, just as she suspected after seeing that truck this morning.

Gracie's first instinct was to run. To get as far away as possible.

She glanced at the ring on her finger.

But running wasn't an option right now.

She sighed. Since she'd arrived at the Community Safety building, she'd mostly been hanging out in Dillon's office. She'd made herself useful for a little while by organizing the break room.

But as she stepped in the hallway to head back to Dillon's office, voices drifted down the corridor.

"So the Fergusons hired someone to trail us?" one of the men asked.

"That's right." Dillon's familiar voice floated through the air. "I talked to this guy last night. They're going to do anything possible to get this resort deal. It wouldn't surprise me if they start paying people off to try to acquire more property."

"I heard rumor they're trying to get around some of the island's laws by building hotels that are technically oversized houses big enough to be hotels," another male said.

"What do you mean?"

Gracie crept closer, curious about the conversation. She didn't want to eavesdrop, but the door was open, and the talk didn't seem to be a secret . . .

"There are certain building codes in place," the first man said. "But if a structure has less than twelve bedrooms then it still qualifies as a house instead of a commercial property, even though it's big enough to be a hotel. It wouldn't surprise me if the Fergusons are planning on building more than one of those 'event houses' so they can get around zoning laws."

"They'll do anything to make sure that their plans succeed," Dillon said.

Curiosity burned inside Gracie. It would be a shame to ruin this island by developing it too much. Sure, people who want to make money would probably jump at the chance to do it here.

But the wild horses roaming Cape Corral needed their space. She could only imagine what would happen with too much automotive traffic.

"We've got to think of a way to stop them," Dillon said.

Gracie cleared her throat and stepped into the room, deciding to own up to the fact she'd been eavesdropping. "I may have an idea for you."

The four men sitting around the table each stared at her.

She licked her lips before launching into her plan.

DILLON STARED AT GRACIE, waiting to hear what the socialite would have to say.

She rubbed her hands on her leggings before starting. "The truth is, I'm a paralegal up in the DC area. We handle a lot of cases, and we've worked for a lot of lobbyists. There was a similar case on the Eastern Shore of Virginia where someone wanted to develop some land on the water. But the firm I worked for was able to stop them."

Dillon crossed his arms, curious about where she was going with this. "How did they do that?"

"It turned out that there was a protected species of bird that liked to nest in that area. Because of that, and because these birds are protected by law, these people weren't allowed to build on this land, even though they'd purchased it. Eventually, the National Park Service bought it back from them, and the land became public property."

Dillon nodded slowly as he chewed on her idea. "That sounds good, but how are we supposed to find out if there are piping plovers or some other protected bird nesting on this property?"

"Some of you guys here work for the forestry service," she said. "I'm sure you can figure it out. Besides, I was just reading some brochures I found on your desk. It looks like there's already a lot of protected wildlife here on the island."

Dillon glanced over at Grant, who worked as one of those forestry officers.

"I think she might have a good idea." Grant nodded slowly. "If we can prove that building on the land is going to be a danger not only to the horses but to other protected species, maybe we can actually have a case we can build on."

Dillon glanced over at Gracie and gave her a nod.

As he did, he saw her cheeks heat in satisfaction.

"Thanks for your help, Gracie," he told her.

She nodded back. "No problem."

CHAPTER TWENTY-THREE

GRACIE CONTINUED to look over her shoulder for the rest of the day. Finally, well after the sun set, she and Dillon went back to his place.

Their place.

Though the day had gone fairly well so far, she dreaded that the evening might hold more awkward conversations.

But at least she would be safe.

For a while.

Maybe.

Gracie couldn't be too certain about these things. Not given the stakes and what she knew about Constantine.

Dillon strode toward the fridge as soon as they

walked inside and poured himself a glass of iced tea. Someone had brought some lunch to them at the station. Gracie had gotten a Caesar salad to hold her over.

"Would you like something to drink?" Dillon asked.

"I'm fine," she barely managed to mutter.

Her appetite was pretty much gone at this point.

"Question." Dillon leaned against the kitchen counter as he addressed her.

"Go ahead."

"Who's running your parents' business now?"

She sat at the kitchen table and let out a breath. "A man named Philip Abram. Why do you ask?"

"Why didn't Constantine go after Philip instead of you? Wouldn't that make more sense?"

"I've thought about that also." Gracie let out another sigh. "But Philip is principled and strong. He's not one Constantine could manipulate. Besides, it doesn't matter what Philip's position is. When I turn thirty in a couple of weeks, the company is mine. Even if Constantine and his guys were able to strongarm Philip into handing control over to them now, it wouldn't matter in the not-so-distant future."

"I suppose that makes sense. But you said they

were able to manipulate your uncle? That he betrayed you?" Dillon took another sip of his tea.

Gracie nodded. "Max isn't really my uncle, just my father's best friend who raised me through my teens. Neither of my parents had any siblings, so custody went to him when they passed away. I really thought that he was in trouble, that his life was in danger. I never imagined he was secretly working with Constantine on this scheme."

"I'm sure that wasn't easy news to stomach."

"Not at all. If I can't trust him, then who can I trust?" Gracie looked at Dillon, not expecting him to step up to the plate. That hadn't been what she was hinting at all. But maybe it was good to get it out there that she'd been burned too badly to fully rely on anyone else.

"I guess my point is that, if Constantine can't get to you, who can he go through in order to get what he wants?" Dillon asked.

Gracie shook her head. "That's the thing. There's no one else."

A knock sounded at the door, the raps cutting through the silence hanging after Gracie's last statement.

Dillon shoved away from the counter and stood between Gracie and the door. "Stay there."

DILLON STRODE toward the door and opened it. He blinked at the person he saw on the other side. "Mom?"

"Surprise!" She reached out and pulled him into a bear hug. "I'm taking three months to pay surprise visits to everyone I love the most. It's your turn!"

"This is certainly a surprise. You weren't supposed to be here until next week." Dillon hadn't had time to come up with a cover story for Gracie yet. He thought he'd had more time.

His mom pulled out of the hug and glanced behind him. Her eyes widened with delight when she spotted Gracie. She quickly sashayed her way.

"And who is this beautiful woman?" his mom asked.

Dillon swallowed hard. This was what he'd wanted—to get his mom off his case about getting married.

But that didn't stop guilt from flooding through him.

He cleared his throat. "Mom . . . this is Gracie . . . my wife."

His mom gasped as she looked at him and then

turned to Gracie. She reached toward Gracie with her arms outstretched and her mouth open.

"Oh, Gracie!" his mom squealed. "Look at you. Aren't you beautiful!"

Gracie's cheeks turned a deep shade of red. "You look just as beautiful as Dillon said as well."

"I wish I could say that Dillon told me about you." His mom looked over her shoulder and scowled. "But he didn't. How could he keep a secret like you all to himself?"

Gracie let out a feeble laugh. "You know Dillon."

"Yes, I do." His mom looped her arm through Gracie's. "We have a lot of catching up to do. Maybe I could make you some of my famous chicken ala king in the process."

"Chicken ala king? That sounds delicious."

"I'll teach you my secret recipe. In fact, I have so much to teach you. I've always wanted a daughter!"

Gracie glanced over at Dillon and smiled.

He ran a hand over his face.

It looked as if his problems had just taken a turn for the worse.

But when he stepped outside to grab his mom's bags, a truck he'd never seen before slowly crept by.

Dillon squinted, trying to see through the

windows. But the sun hit them, making it impossible to see inside.

All he could think about was—what if Constantine was behind the wheel?

What if the man was still trying to stake out the island for Gracie?

CHAPTER TWENTY-FOUR

GRACIE HAD a great time getting to know Dillon's mom—Marla, as she'd insisted Gracie call her.

The woman was gregarious, fun, and warm—everything Dillon wasn't.

Apparently, Dillon had been more like his father, who'd passed away from cancer nearly ten years ago. He'd been serious, reserved, and quiet.

For the first time in a long time, Gracie almost felt like she was a part of a real family. For a moment, she'd seen herself fitting in. Being loved.

Being someone other than an orphan.

All these years since her parents' deaths, and Gracie still felt that way. Like she was all alone. Like she'd lost the only people who truly had her back.

The thought caused resounding sadness to echo inside her.

Even with Constantine's family . . . when things had seemed good between them . . . she'd never felt accepted.

At nine p.m., Marla announced she was ready for bed.

Dillon's gaze shot over to Gracie.

She knew exactly what he was thinking.

He only had one spare bedroom, and Gracie's stuff was in it.

She jumped to her feet and glanced at Marla. "You know what? I left a few things in the guest bedroom. You know how us women are . . . we always have enough clothes to fill several closets! Let me grab some stuff, change the sheets, and the room will be all yours."

"Change the sheets?" Marla raised an eyebrow.

Panic raced through Gracie. She hated lying. *Hated* it. But what other choice did she have right now?

"I . . . uh . . . I slept in there one night when I wasn't feeling well," Gracie said. "There was no need to keep Dillon up."

"I see." Marla nodded, seeming to buy Gracie's

story. "That's no problem. Do you want me to help you?"

"I've got it," Gracie insisted. "You just enjoy some time with your son."

Quickly, Gracie hurried back to the room and grabbed the few belongings to her name.

She hesitated as she stared at the door to Dillon's room.

They were going to have to figure something out for the night.

She dreaded what that might be.

AS SOON AS his mom went to bed, Dillon glanced at Gracie.

He knew the exhaustion in her gaze matched the exhaustion he felt.

What a long day.

A long couple of days.

Yet, despite his exhaustion, Dillon knew he was nowhere close to turning in for the night. He had too much on his mind.

He also knew he'd have to deal with the sleeping arrangements, and he hoped to delay that conversation for a while.

"How would you like to go outside for a bonfire?" he asked Gracie instead.

Bonfires were one of his favorite ways to unwind and sort through his thoughts.

Gracie's eyebrows shot up, as if the invitation surprised her, before she finally shrugged. "Why not?"

Gracie followed Dillon outside and sat on a metal gliding loveseat that Dillon had placed in front of the stone-encased pit.

He'd already prepared the firewood last time he was out here. All he had to do was pull out a starter brick and light it. A few minutes later, flames licked the edges of the wood. The blaze already felt good, especially since the air was chillier now that the sun had disappeared.

Dillon settled on the glider near Gracie—careful not to get too close—and handed her a blanket he'd brought out. It was chillier outside than he'd expected.

Gracie pulled her knees to her chest as she stared at the flames. "So, I've been meaning to ask . . . does everyone here on this island dress like a cowboy?"

A smile danced across his lips. He was grateful for the lighthearted conversation. "What can I say?

When in Rome . . ."

Gracie chuckled. "I see."

"Honestly, there's more to the cowboy getup than you might think."

"Please enlighten me then."

"The cowboy hat keeps the sun out of your eyes," he explained. "And cowboy boots are easy to slide into the stirrups when you're riding, plus they protect your feet from being crushed—just in case a horse was to step on you or something."

"It's starting to make sense then. Maybe I can stop thinking that all you guys are having some kind of grown-up costume party."

He chuckled this time. "You're funny."

"Not so much anymore." Her smile faded. "What do you guys do for fun around here?"

"Besides the beach? We keep ourselves occupied. There's fishing and boating. We eat at The Screen Porch Café and have social events at a place called Smith's Hope. Sometimes, the kids take sleds and race down the sand dunes."

"That sounds fun."

"It's a great place to raise a family, even if our school is only one room."

"Those still exist?"

"They do."

"That is incredible."

"Oh, and I should have mentioned that my friend Wade—he's a volunteer firefighter—set up some target rings in his backyard so we can have ax-throwing contests."

"Interesting."

"And a few of us are brushing up on our lassoing skills."

"Lassoing skills?"

Dillon shrugged. "You never know when they might come in handy."

"I suppose you're right." A moment of silence passed before Gracie said, "Your mom seems really great."

With that sentence, the conversation turned more serious—as Dillon knew it inevitably would. "She is. She's one in a million."

"I'm sorry you're in this position." Gracie's voice dipped low with regret. "I feel like it's my fault."

"It's not your fault, Gracie. I'm a grown man. I made this decision just as well as you did."

"It feels like my fault. If you hadn't met me, none of this would have happened."

Dillon turned toward Gracie as the fire crackled in front of them. "Listen, I suppose I should explain about my first marriage. It didn't end well."

She glanced at him, curiosity in her gaze. "I'm sorry to hear that. What happened?"

He let out a long breath. "Before I came here to Cape Corral, I was in the military for about eight years. When I was at home from deployment, I met Lauren. It was one of those insta-love moments. We met and were married three months later."

"Wow—that is fast. Not that we have any room to talk, I suppose." Gracie seemed to clamp her mouth shut.

"A year after we were married, I deployed for six months. When I came home, Lauren had left. Said she couldn't handle the military life. Didn't try to help make things better or find any solutions. She'd made up her mind, and she was gone."

"I'm sorry. I can only imagine how difficult that would have been."

"It was. I didn't expect it from her. Some people might think, because we were only together for such a short amount of time, that it shouldn't have been that big of a deal. But it was to me. I planned on forever with her."

"I bet. Is that how you ended up coming here?"

He shifted, still staring at the fire. "When I got out of the military, I knew I wanted to do something different with my life. I'd always been interested in firefighting. I'd visited this place before and fell in love with the island. When I heard that they were looking for two full-time firefighters, I applied. Now here I am."

"That's great. But this whole island only has two firefighters?"

"Full time. We have about twelve volunteers. We also have Sanctuary Watchers who help us monitor the horses. People don't mind stepping up, even if there's no financial gain involved. They do it because it's the right thing."

"That's . . . great."

He nodded. "I like it here. It's a slower pace of life, but it's good."

The glider slid back and forth, back and forth, back and forth. The motion was soothing, as was the fire.

Dillon kept an eye on everything around him, making sure there were no visitors.

He was well aware that Constantine could be here on the island.

This man could know where Gracie was.

Which meant that Dillon would have to be even more on guard than usual.

CHAPTER TWENTY-FIVE

GRACIE ENJOYED the brief moment of tranquility as she and Dillon chatted, almost like two normal people getting to know each other. The conversation gave her hope that being here wouldn't be as horrible as she thought.

She stared at the crackling fire and pulled the blanket up higher around her shoulders.

Who would have ever thought that being in a place that had started with anguish could turn into a peaceful moment like this?

"Good job back there at the station," Dillon said quietly. "I didn't realize you were a paralegal."

Gracie nodded. "I quit my job about a month ago so I could prepare to transition to working for my parents' company. Truthfully, I actually wanted to be a lawyer, but I settled for being a paralegal instead."

"Why didn't you take your education any further?"

She tugged the blanket again as she considered her response. "It kind of sounds strange, but Max said I was better off not taking that many years of schooling."

Dillon's eyebrows shot together. "Why would he say that?"

Gracie shrugged. "At the time, I was struggling to believe in myself. Losing my parents . . . it was hard. My life . . . it was so different."

"I can only imagine."

"So when Max said I wasn't cut out to be a lawyer, it only seemed to confirm that I wasn't smart enough for law school. It was a shame, really, because I thought a degree in law would help me at my parents' company."

"Did you ever work for your parents' company?"

Gracie nodded. "I interned there in college. But Philip, the CEO, tried to mentor me. Said I was better off getting some real-world experience and then, when the time came, he'd show me the ropes."

"So what did you do?"

"I became a paralegal."

"I see."

"The truth is, for most of my life, people have underestimated me. They see my blonde hair and cheerful disposition, and they think I'm an airhead. Most people didn't believe that I was going to grow up to be anything more than someone who married somebody wealthy and lived happily ever after."

"That's not what you wanted?"

She shook her head. "It's not. I wanted to use this feistiness I have inside me to do some good."

"You know, it's never too late."

His voice sounded so low and sincere that a shiver went down her spine.

Gracie nodded, trying to imagine herself taking law school classes while here on Cape Corral. It looked like she had just nipped that dream in the bud.

But there was something else on her mind right now also, something more important than that. "I never saw it at the time, but now I have to wonder if Max was grooming me for what was going to happen."

Dillon turned toward her. "What do you mean?"

"I mean, I just wondered if Max wanted me to doubt myself because he knew it would be easier to control me in the end. I think he's wanted to gain control of my father's company for a long time also. He saw me as a way to do that."

Dillon didn't say anything. He just looked at her with a mesmerizing look in his eyes—a look that seemed to see into her very soul.

She expected judgment—but she saw none.

"Truthfully, Constantine was the same way," Gracie continued. "Whenever I tried to rise to an occasion, he was quick to push me back down, to put me in my place."

Dillon's fingers brushed her shoulder. "I think you have a spirit that's going to let you do whatever you set your mind to, Gracie."

Her heart pounded in her chest at his words.

She'd craved hearing those words for so long.

She never dreamed that she would hear them from the cowboy she'd conveniently married.

SOMETHING ABOUT GRACIE'S words got to Dillon.

As they sat there with the bonfire crackling in front of them, the faint glow of flames illuminated her face. When mixed with the plaid blanket she had pulled up high around her shoulders . . . the sight of it did something to Dillon's heart. Something he hadn't expected.

He wasn't supposed to be attracted to this woman. He *definitely* wasn't supposed to *like* this woman. But more than anything, he wasn't supposed to be tempted to kiss her.

That's exactly what Dillon was thinking about doing right now.

But he wouldn't.

Even if Gracie was his wife.

That word still felt foreign on his lips.

But he knew he couldn't let himself think about that fact for too long or he might feel antsy. He might realize the long-term meaning of that word. He might think through too many negative possibilities.

After staring at the fire until the flames began to die, and Dillon knew it was time to go to bed.

The moment he dreaded.

"I know the situation right now isn't ideal, but I'll sleep on the floor," he started. "I had no intentions of us staying in the same room. You know that, right?"

"Having my own room was part of our agreement." Gracie frowned. "But I know it would seem suspicious to your mom if we stayed in separate rooms or if you slept on the couch." She raised a finger almost comically. "No funny business."

Dillon fought a smile. "No funny business."

She stared at him another moment before nodding. "Okay then."

But as they stood, Dillon heard a stick crack in the distance.

His arm shot around Gracie's waist, and he nudged her behind him.

He scanned the woods in the distance.

Was someone out there?

Or had that been a wild animal?

He couldn't be sure.

"Dillon?" Gracie whispered.

"Let's get you inside," he told her. "Now."

Maybe it was a good thing that Gracie was staying in his room.

Because that way, Dillon could better keep her safe.

CHAPTER TWENTY-SIX

AS GRACIE LISTENED to Dillon tossing and turning on the floor, she suppressed a groan.

Why did she feel guilty about this?

Probably because she was the one who'd gotten him into this.

She knew that was the truth.

And maybe because she'd actually felt like the two of them had bonded for a minute tonight while out there by the fire.

He wasn't a muscle-bound cowboy without a soul. No, he was a real person with a real story and real . . . feelings?

The concept seemed foreign when she thought about Dillon.

"Listen." Gracie leaned over the edge of the bed. "Do you have any painter's tape?"

Dillon's eyes popped open, and he stared at her in the darkness. "Painter's tape? Why in the world are you asking about painter's tape in the middle of the night?"

"Because . . . if we put a piece of it down the middle of the bed, maybe you could have one half, and I could have the other."

He said nothing for a minute until finally chuckling. "Thanks, but no thanks, Gracie."

"What? I feel bad. I don't know how long your mom is going to be here, but you can't sleep on the floor for an extended period of time."

He turned over and jerked the blanket over his shoulders. "I'll be fine."

"But will you?"

"Good night, Gracie."

"Don't say I didn't offer."

Dillon only grunted in response.

PAINTER'S TAPE?

Was Gracie out of her mind?

Another part of Dillon wanted to laugh.

CAPE CORRAL KEEPER   191

How could the woman be so infuriating yet so cute at the same time?

But how much longer *could* he sleep on the floor?

It didn't matter. He was going to make it work.

His mom wasn't supposed to be here right now.

Dillon didn't want to feel guilty about it, but he did. Even though he was legitimately married, he knew that, in his heart, nothing about this arrangement was legitimate. The urge to come clean dominated his thoughts.

But what would his mom think if she knew the truth? Certainly, she'd be disappointed—not only at Dillon's actions but also because she genuinely seemed to like Gracie.

Before he could think more about it, his phone buzzed. It was Colby.

Dillon stepped from the room before answering. If his colleague was calling this late, then something was probably up.

"Hey, Boss," Colby started. "I talked to Mr. Dunleavy today when I went over to drop his boat and his check off."

"Okay."

"I thought you'd be interested to know . . . Mr. Dunleavy told me that, not one, but two different men stopped by asking him about his stolen boat."

Dillon's back muscles tightened. "Did he say who?"

"One he identified as the man who's been on TV looking for his missing fiancé."

Dillon swallowed hard. "And?"

"And the second man, he didn't recognize. Said he was looking for someone he knew and thought she might have taken the boat."

"Could he describe him?"

"Said it was too dark," Colby said.

"Thanks, Colby." Dillon ended the call and stood there a minute.

Two people? What sense did that make?

Had Constantine and one of his lackeys both come around asking about Gracie? Were they not communicating with each other? Or was there something else at play here?

He didn't know. But it was something he needed to seriously think about.

A few minutes later, he went back into his room and lay down on his mat. As he did, he glanced up at Gracie.

She appeared to be asleep. A wisp of moonlight from the window hit her face, giving her an angelic glow.

Angelic? Was Dillon out of his mind?

But she'd surprised him tonight.

There was more to the woman than what appeared on the surface. Gracie was smart and determined. Sensitive yet feisty.

Dillon had never really met anyone like her.

Part of him was fascinated.

But all he really needed to concentrate on right now was keeping her safe—especially when considering what Colby had just told him.

There was a good chance this Constantine guy was on this island and that he was looking for her.

Dillon needed to make sure this guy was apprehended.

Then he would figure out the next steps concerning his future.

CHAPTER TWENTY-SEVEN

I'M GETTING CLOSER, Gracie Loveland. So, so close.

He sat in his truck and stared into the darkness around him.

He would find Gracie.

He was tracking her scent like a dog hunting prey.

People didn't think he was the type to do something like this, but he was. He was shrewd when he needed to be. Determined. Crafty.

He was whatever he needed to be whenever he wanted to be.

Gracie wasn't going to stop him from getting what he wanted.

He knew she was on Cape Corral somewhere.

Wherever she hid, he'd find her.

He was getting close.

So close.

He could practically smell her scent in the air.

That man was helping her, wasn't he?

Dillon McGrath.

He'd put things together. All it took was asking a few people around town, and he'd discovered that Gracie had almost been arrested.

Oh, how the locals loved to talk.

That was why he broke into the Community Safety building.

It wasn't hard.

And he'd found what he needed.

He'd found proof—her wedding dress.

Afterward, he'd set Phase Two of his plan into action.

He nearly salivated as he glanced out his window and saw the ocean churning in the distance. Thankfully, he'd found a place to use while he was here.

He'd called in some connections with friends. Even though he drove around now, looking for answers, he would have a place to lay his head tonight.

Everything was working out in his favor.

Just as it always did.

And Gracie wasn't going to change that.

CHAPTER TWENTY-EIGHT

"EVER SINCE DILLON was old enough to talk, all he wanted to do was save the world," Marla said as she and Gracie made a pie together the next day.

"Is that right?" Gracie stirred the apple filling, the scent of sugar and buttery pastry floating through the air and making her stomach rumble.

"He joined the military right out of high school. I hated to see him go, but I didn't want to hold him back either. When he got out, he wanted to come here, of all places."

"I know you must miss him."

"I do. But I want my son to be happy. That's what's important to me. I'm retired now from teaching—I put in twenty-five years—so I can drive here to see Dillon whenever I want. But I can't tell you how much better it makes me feel to know that he has a good woman watching out for him."

Guilt pounded at Gracie's temples. Technically, Dillon *did* have a good woman looking out for him. But, in matters of the heart, the issue was murky.

"So, tell me all about your wedding," Marla said as she rolled out the crust on the counter.

Gracie's spoon nearly went flying from the bowl as she stirred the filling a little too hard. Apples splattered all over the white cabinets, and she cringed.

"I must have gotten you all excited." Marla chuckled and grabbed a dishcloth to help.

Gracie quickly put the bowl down and grabbed some paper towels.

"I guess so." Gracie let out a nervous laugh.

"So?" Marla didn't forget her question as she grabbed some spray cleaner.

"It was really sweet." Gracie licked her lips as she tossed her paper towel full of sugar-coated fruit in the trash. "It was simple and pretty fast—for most people, at least. We went to the church, and I wore a simple sundress—"

"He wore a white button-up shirt and called himself dressed up, didn't he?"

Gracie smiled. "He did. I didn't mind. We only

had a few people there, but I've always wanted a small ceremony. It was . . . beautiful. Dillon was very sweet."

Marla's face beamed with pride. "That's my boy. What can I say? He's always been a hero."

"Yes, he is." Gracie's voice caught.

Gracie had probably been too harsh on the man. It was hard when every male she'd ever met treated her as if she was beneath them. Or like she was just eye candy. Or like her brain and opinions didn't matter.

When Gracie had first seen Dillon, those had been her assumptions too. Someone as macho as him certainly carried those same kinds of beliefs in him.

But maybe she'd been too quick to judge. After all, the man had been through a lot. Gracie couldn't stop thinking about his ex-wife.

Almost as if Marla could read her thoughts, she brought the subject up. "I like you a lot better than I liked Lauren."

Gracie had to admit that she was curious about Dillon's first wife. "You didn't like her, huh?"

"From the moment I met her, I thought she was flighty and all wrong for my son. I was right."

"It was wrong what she did to him."

Marla paused and turned to Gracie, something changing in her gaze. "But you? I just look at you, and I know you're going to be in my life for a long time."

Gracie's breath caught. What did she even say to that? Could Marla see the truth in her gaze—the truth that they'd gotten married for every reason but love?

Before Gracie had a chance to respond, a news story from the TV in the other room caught her ear.

Her blood went cold.

Constantine's voice floated over the airwaves.

Gracie couldn't let Marla hear whatever he had to say, or the woman could realize the truth of her and Dillon's relationship.

Instead, Gracie looked at Dillon's mom and offered a huge grin. "You know what I like to do when I bake? I like to sing *Mary Poppins* songs at the top of my lungs."

Before Marla could say anything else, Gracie began belting "Spoonful of Sugar."

If only she had an umbrella to help her fly away.

DILLON WALKED into his house in time to hear Gracie acting out a musical in the kitchen with his mom.

What was going on?

At least the scent of apples and cinnamon floated through the air. Things could be worse.

Maybe.

Gracie stopped mid-verse when she spotted Dillon, and she plastered on a smile.

She looked like the picture of a happy housewife wearing a dress and an apron.

Dress? Dillon didn't remember Gracie buying herself one of those at the store yesterday.

Almost as if she'd read his thoughts, Gracie held out the skirt of the floral-print outfit. "Don't you like it? Your mom whipped it up for me this morning using some material she brought to make throw pillows. Can you believe it?"

Dillon smiled. That shouldn't surprise him. "It looks nice."

"She is just delightful, Dillon," his mom quipped as she put some lattice over a pie. "We've had the best time working together today. Thanksgiving is going to be extra special this year."

"It looks and smells like it." Dillon glanced around and saw flour scattered on surfaces across his kitchen. His sink was full of dishes. Various ingredients were scattered on the counter.

Something about the moment felt a little too normal.

"Can I talk to you for a minute, Gracie?" Dillon wished that he could just enjoy this lighthearted slice of life. But he couldn't.

"Of course." She wiped her hands on a dish towel before joining him. He nodded down the hallway. "In private."

"You two don't be too long." His mom giggled.

Dillon wanted to shake his head, but he kept his expression placid instead. He put his hand on Gracie's back as he led her to the bedroom where they could talk privately.

Once inside, he closed the door and lowered himself on one side of the bed. Gracie sat on the other side.

"What's going on?" she asked, her fingers knitting together in her lap.

"Constantine was just on TV again today," he started.

"I know." Gracie scowled. "Why do you think I was singing so loud? I didn't want your mom to hear what he was saying."

"Smart thinking . . . I guess." That explained her strange antics.

"What did he say?" Gracie rushed.

"I thought you might want to see for yourself." Dillon pulled out his phone and found the news footage.

Gracie scooted closer so she could see. As she did, Dillon caught a whiff of her flowery shampoo. The aroma was nice—a little too nice.

He quickly snapped back to the present. This was no time to think about how wonderful Gracie smelled. That wouldn't get him anywhere.

Instead, he braced himself for Gracie's reaction to this footage.

Constantine appeared on the screen, a river behind him as well as some tall office buildings. Every dirty-blond hair was in place, his dress shirt looked impeccably pressed, and his classic features showed no flaw.

But his eyes . . . they were red-rimmed.

He was an excellent faker, apparently.

"Was this filmed this morning?" Gracie's voice caught.

"It appears."

She straightened. "That means he's not here in

Cape Corral. Maybe I was wrong when I saw that truck drive by."

"That's true. Maybe he's not. That's one piece of good news."

Gracie's eyes went still before she looked back at the screen, almost as if she sensed something bad was coming.

Constantine spoke to the camera. "I'm still looking for my fiancée. Her name is Gracie Loveland, and, like I said yesterday, I don't believe that she's in her right mind."

"What do you mean?" the reporter asked. "Is she a danger to others?"

Constantine shook his head, a torn, confused expression sketched onto the lines of his tight face. "I wouldn't say that. Gracie has a good heart, but she has a lot of problems. She never fully dealt with her parents' deaths. I begged her to get help, but she wasn't interested. As a result of that, sometimes she can be . . . unstable, let's say. That's what worries me right now."

Dillon felt Gracie tense beside him.

He hit Off on the video and turned to her. When he did, he saw the moisture in her eyes. Compassion surged through him.

"Gracie . . ."

She shook her head and looked away, probably before he could see her tears.

"Don't let what he said get to you," Dillon said.

"It's just . . . I've always felt like I was meant for so much more than that."

Against his better instincts, Dillon reached forward and squeezed her arm. To his surprise, Gracie didn't pull away.

"You can do whatever you want to do," he told her. "I see it in the fire in your eyes."

She swung her gaze up to meet his. "You're just being nice."

"No one has ever accused me of that before," Dillon assured her. "I'm certainly not changing for you now."

A hesitant smile fluttered across her face before disappearing.

But Dillon saw more moisture in her gaze, and his heart swelled with compassion.

As Gracie looked up at him, Dillon somehow found himself wrapping his arms around her and pulling her close. She looked like she needed someone to be there for her right now. She had no one here on this island.

No one but him.

It was amazing how well she fit into his arms. How her head could tuck under his chin.

He could get used to this—

Dillon's phone rang, and he pulled away, instantly missing Gracie's warmth. But when he saw Grant was calling, Dillon knew he had to take it. This could be important.

"What's going on?" he answered.

"I thought you'd want to know that the missing wedding dress turned up."

Dillon tensed, waiting to see where this was going to go. "Where?"

"It was found in a parking lot down in Nags Head."

Why had someone stolen the gown just to take it to a parking lot a couple of towns south? Before Dillon could ask the question, Grant continued.

"The strange thing is that there was blood on the dress and a note was left with it."

Dillon glanced at Gracie, wondering how she would react to this news. "What did the note say?"

"In summary? It said she couldn't handle the pressure anymore. She apologized to her fiancé for leaving him at the altar and said she wouldn't be trouble to anybody anymore this side of heaven. It was signed, Gracie Loveland."

CHAPTER TWENTY-NINE

I WON'T BE trouble for anybody anymore this side of heaven.

The words kept replaying in Gracie's mind. She had no doubt Constantine had chosen those words on purpose.

He'd wanted to send a message—a message that she wouldn't be around anymore.

Not only that, but he wanted to make it look like Gracie really was unstable and losing her mind.

What would he try next? Since he'd stolen the wedding dress, did that mean Constantine knew she was here? And, if that was the case, what was he planning?

Dillon stared at Gracie as they sat on the edge of the bed. "You okay?"

Gracie had to give him credit because he actually sounded like he cared. "I'll be fine. Really."

He gave her another hesitant glance. "I need to get back to work, unfortunately. Are you going to be okay to stay here?"

She nodded. "Of course."

"I want you to keep all the doors locked and not to answer unless it's me. Understand?"

Gracie nodded again. "Absolutely."

He stared at her for another moment before rising. "We're going to find some answers for you."

"I appreciate that. Thank you again. I'm just going to stay in here for a few more minutes, if that's okay. I need to collect myself."

"Of course."

As Dillon left her alone, Gracie's heart pounded in her ears. She had no idea what the outcome of all this would be, nor did she like the possibilities that floated through her head.

Constantine wasn't done with her. Not by any means. She hated sitting back and not doing anything.

As soon as she heard the front door close and Dillon's truck pull away, Gracie walked from the room. Marla was cleaning up the kitchen, and the pies were in the oven.

Gracie stopped beside her, trying to keep her voice even. "I have a weird question, but my phone is totally dead. I wondered if I might be able to use yours?"

"Well, yes, of course!"

Look relaxed, Gracie reminded herself.

The last thing she needed was for Marla to see through her.

Marla grabbed her cell from her purse and handed it to Gracie. "Here you go!"

"Thank you," Gracie said. "I'll only be a minute."

Gripping the phone, she escaped back to her room again. As soon as the door was closed, she dialed Philip's number.

Philip would know what to do. He was the most level-headed person Gracie had ever met.

Even though the two of them weren't especially close, he would be a good sounding board for this situation. Maybe she should have gone to him earlier. But her thoughts had felt so muddy.

Gracie desperately needed someone to talk to right now. Since being with Constantine, a divide had formed between her and her friends. Gracie hadn't seen the separation at the time. But now it made perfect sense. Constantine had been trying to isolate her, and it had worked.

Never again, Gracie vowed.

She'd dialed Philip's cell phone, but there was no answer.

She frowned and looked at the phone another moment. Had Philip not answered because he didn't recognize this number?

It was a possibility.

Gracie could leave a message, but she didn't want to risk that.

Instead, she tried one more tactic.

She dialed the number to Philip's office.

She lowered her voice so no one would recognize her as she said, "I'm trying to reach Philip Abram. I am calling about his business loan with the United American Bank."

Gracie knew her words were believable—she knew enough about the company to know what bank they used.

"I'm sorry, but he's not in the office today," the woman on the other end said.

"This matter is rather urgent," Gracie said. "Do you know when he'll be back in?"

"Unfortunately, I haven't heard from him today. But I'll try his cell phone to see if I can reach him."

Philip hadn't come into the office today, *and* he wasn't answering his cell phone.

A bad feeling brewed in Gracie's gut.

That wasn't like the CEO.

Not at all.

"WE'LL DEFINITELY KEEP our eyes open for anyone suspicious," Grant said after Dillon explained the situation to his coworkers. He'd told them everything—there was no reason to hold back. They'd gathered around a table at the station to discuss what was going on.

"The Nags Head PD will test the dress to see what type of blood was found on it," Dash added. "But that could take a couple of days."

"We're going to need to tell the other police departments what's going on," Grant added. "As much as I would like to keep this quiet, these other investigations will be impacted, and we can't withhold evidence from them. I'd expect them to extend the courtesy to us if the roles were reversed."

"I just don't want Gracie to be in any more danger," Dillon said.

Grant frowned. "I understand. I really do."

"You're talking about telling them about the dress and letting authorities know to end the missing person's search?" Dillon's gut tightened. It wasn't ideal, but he understood where Grant was coming from.

"It's the right thing to do." Grant shrugged, almost apologetically. "I might be able to buy a little time—a few hours at most."

"Do that. The more space we have, the more I can do to make sure Gracie is safe."

Grant nodded. "Consider it done."

Silence fell for a minute.

"Seems like we can't catch a break here on the island lately, doesn't it?" Dash added with a shrug.

"Tell me about it," Dillon muttered. Several suspicious things had happened over the past several months. He'd hoped those incidents were behind them, but apparently not. "Any updates on this PJ guy?"

Grant tapped his pen against the table. "Last I heard, he was going door to door and trying to drum up support for this new resort. He's even handing out signs that people can put in their yards to show they're in favor of this change. It's all catawampus, if you ask me."

"Those signs sound like something else that will eventually become litter or a hazard to the horses." Dillon's jaw flexed at the thought.

"My thoughts exactly." Grant stood, stretching his back. "But right now, this man isn't doing anything illegal. There is nothing we can do to stop him."

"And he knows that." Dillon shook his head. "The good news is that Gracie has connections with some magazines. She thinks she'll be able to run a story about the wild horses on the island—a story that will emphasize how important it is that this area remains undeveloped."

"That's great news," Dash said. "Sounds like just what we need."

"That's what I'm hoping," Dillon said. "We need something to counteract the big magazine spread done by *Carolina Coast Monthly*."

His friends left a few minutes later, and Dillon stared at his computer. On a whim, he typed in Constantine's name.

After he looked through everything he could find about the man, he then turned to the man's family.

Gracie was right. The man's brother—Angelino —did have some political aspirations. On social media, Angelino talked about how he was thinking about running for Congress.

As he stared at the man's pictures, his phone rang.

It was one of Dillon's contacts with the FBI whom he'd called earlier.

"Hey, man," Franco started. "I wanted to share what I learned with you."

Dillon sat up straighter. "I'd love for something to work in my favor right now."

"Maybe this will do the trick. It turns out that Constantine's brother Angelino has some shady things in his past. He's covered them up, for the most part. There's nothing you'd find on the internet. But word on the street is that the DiMarzio family is in the weapons-smuggling business."

"And using their pillow business as a disguise?"

"You know it. It's an active investigation right now. You can't tell anyone I told you this."

"It's between you and me. Thanks for your help."

"No problem. I'd stay away from the family, if I were you. They're no good. You know that bride that went missing is connected with them too, right?"

Dillon frowned. "I heard that. Thanks again for your help."

He ended the call.

This situation ran much deeper than Dillon had ever imagined. It was more than about Constantine wanting to take over a media empire. If he got his hands on White Star, he could use it for either political advantage or as some means for their smuggling operation.

The stakes had just gotten even more serious.

And Gracie remained caught in the crossfire.

CHAPTER THIRTY

AS SOON AS Dillon got back to the house that evening, Gracie, Marla, and Dillon sat down to eat the meal Marla had taught Gracie how to prepare. Tonight's menu was pot roast with homemade mashed potatoes, green beans, and biscuits.

If Gracie kept eating this way, she was going to gain twenty pounds. But the food tasted so great—just the comfort she needed.

They had friendly chitchat afterward.

"So tell me, I've already heard about your wedding, but I haven't heard how the two of you met," Marla said as she cut up a piece of roast.

Gracie felt her lungs tighten, and she glanced at Dillon.

He said nothing.

Finally, Gracie cleared her throat. "Dillon actually saved me."

Marla's eyebrows shot up. "Saved you? Tell me more."

"I foolishly took a boat out when I shouldn't have. I got caught in a bad situation and fell overboard. Dillon rescued me and . . . we've been together ever since."

Gracie didn't bother to mention that had only been a couple of days ago.

"What a wonderful love story." Marla clasped her hands together beneath her chin. "Just imagine telling your kids that one day."

Gracie nearly choked on her sip of sweet tea. Kids? They were *not* a part of this plan.

Nope.

Even though, at one point in her life, Gracie *had* wanted children.

She supposed that dream would never come to fruition now, would it?

A surprising disappointment filled her.

Dillon patted her back. "Are you okay, honey?"

She pointed to her throat. "My drink just went down the wrong way."

"I'm sorry to hear that."

She stood and fanned her face. "Actually, if you'll

excuse me a minute. I don't want to cough at the table."

Dillon's eyes twinkled as he looked up at her. "Of course."

"And, one more thing . . . could I use your cell phone, honey? Mine still isn't working."

The twinkle in Dillon's eyes quickly turned into a smolder. He made it clear he had no idea what she was up to and that he didn't like it.

"Sure." He pulled it from his pocket and handed it to her, unlocking it first.

Then Gracie excused herself and went back to the bedroom.

She closed the door and leaned against it as she dialed Philip's number again.

She almost didn't expect him to answer.

But on the fourth ring, he did.

Or, she should say, *someone* did.

"I'm trying to reach Philip," she stuttered.

"Who is this?"

"Who is this?" she countered.

"This is Evan."

"Evan?" Evan was the senior vice president of White Star. Gracie had always liked the man with his quiet ways and his dedication to his family.

"That's right. Who is this?" Evan asked again.

"Oh . . . I'm sorry. I'm Louise. I'm with the bank, and I've been trying to reach Philip all day," Gracie managed to say. "I know I'm calling after hours, but I had no luck trying to get in touch with him earlier today, and it's urgent that I speak with him."

"Philip isn't home," Evan said. "We don't know where he is."

"But you're answering his cell?" The question escaped before Gracie could stop it.

"If you must know, yes. He didn't take his phone with him."

"But he always takes—" Gracie stopped herself. "I mean, it seems like most people always take their cell phones with them."

"That's why everyone is a little concerned. Now, I'm sorry, but I can't talk right now. Right now, I need to find Philip."

Gracie ended the call and pulled the cell phone toward her. She held it to her chest as she processed what she'd just learned.

What if Constantine or one of his guys had grabbed Philip when they realized they couldn't get Gracie?

What if he was now in danger?

WHEN GRACIE DIDN'T APPEAR from the bedroom after several minutes, Dillon headed that way. Something was up. He was certain of it.

He lightly knocked on the door before twisting the handle.

"Gracie?" he called. "Mom is getting worried. Everything okay?"

As soon as he stepped in and saw the look on her face, Dillon knew something was wrong.

He shut the door and turned toward her. "What's going on?"

Gracie's big eyes stared up at him. "It's Philip . . . he's missing."

"Philip?"

"He's the CEO of my parents' company. I've been trying to reach him today."

Surprise coursed through Dillon. "Why would you do that? Do you want people to know you're here?"

Her eyes narrowed. "I didn't tell anyone who answered that it was me. I had a cover story, and I made sure to lower my voice."

At least she'd thought of that, Dillon mused. He still wasn't sure any of it was a good idea, though.

"Besides, I . . . I just needed someone familiar to talk to," Gracie said.

Dillon lowered himself on the edge of the bed. "So tell me more about this Philip guy."

"He's a good man, and he's done a great job with the company. He's the kind of guy who lives for his career. He's not even married, and he doesn't have children. He loves what he does too much. He even said that once. It's not like him to be anywhere without a cell phone."

"But you're saying that's what is going on right now?"

"He hasn't answered all day. Finally, someone picked up, but it was the senior vice president of White Star. Evan said that Philip hasn't been seen all day, and he left his cell phone at home."

Dillon felt the tension pull at his muscles. "So you think Constantine got him?"

Gracie's gaze met his. "It's my best guess."

CHAPTER THIRTY-ONE

GRACIE SQUEEZED HER EYES SHUT, only one thought echoing in her head.

Wherever she was, danger would be.

That was becoming more and more clear to her with every moment that passed.

She pulled the blanket up higher around her shoulders and dug her head into the soft pillow. It was dark in the room, and Dillon appeared to be sleeping soundly on the floor.

Gracie had turned in early for the night. There was no way that she was going to be able to fake everything in front of Marla. So she'd feigned having a headache.

But really, Gracie just couldn't stop thinking about Philip.

If Constantine and his guys had grabbed him, then what else would they do?

Even worse, what if they found out she was here and went after Marla?

Gracie would never forgive herself if that happened.

This whole scheme had seemed to make sense at one time. But now that Gracie was digging deeper into things, she realized what a mistake this was. Dillon and Marla had accepted her into their lives, and now she was putting them at risk.

Her problems were not *their* problems. She'd never be able to live with herself if she continued on like this.

A plan settled in her mind.

Tomorrow, when Dillon was at work, Gracie would make up an excuse for getting out of the house. Then she'd somehow figure out a way to leave Cape Corral before she caused any more damage.

Did she believe that marriage was for life?

Absolutely.

Maybe one day, when this all passed, Gracie would come back here and make things right.

But the kindest thing that she could do right now

was to put as much space as possible between herself and everyone here.

Sadness pressed on her at the thought.

But Gracie still knew it was for the best.

———

DILLON TURNED over on the little mat he'd spread across the floor to sleep on.

No way would he be able to rest tonight.

But Gracie thought he was sleeping.

He only knew because, as soon as he'd gone still, he'd heard her sniffle.

She was crying.

Dillon couldn't blame her for being upset over what had happened to Philip. Over the fact that he was missing.

Dillon had gotten Grant to put in a few phone calls about it, and everything Gracie had said was confirmed.

There was now a missing person alert out for the man up in the DC area.

As Dillon heard Gracie sniffle again, his heart pounded harder.

Part of him wanted to comfort her.

But he knew that would be a bad idea. Any gestures like that would most likely not be welcome.

But Dillon's heart went out to the woman.

Yes, Gracie could be extremely aggravating. But she also had a good heart. The fact that people constantly underestimated her only made Dillon want to stand up for her more.

But what he really had to figure out was a way to help her.

He'd put in a few calls with his friends outside the area to see if they knew anything about this Constantine guy. He hadn't heard back yet.

He also wanted more information on that wedding dress. Certainly, the note from Gracie that had been forged had been done carefully.

I won't be trouble for anybody anymore this side of heaven was the main line that continued to echo in his head.

Someone had been trying to send a message. A *threatening* message.

These people wouldn't stop until Gracie was somehow under their control.

Or until she was dead.

Dillon didn't like either of those thoughts.

Nor was he going to let either of those things happen.

CHAPTER THIRTY-TWO

TODAY WOULD BE the perfect day to leave, Gracie realized the next morning as she brushed her teeth.

Marla had decided to go to Nags Head to do some shopping. She was going with Emmy, who was taking a trip that way anyway. They'd invited Gracie, but she'd told them she still had a headache.

All night, Gracie had thought about her plan to run. Leaving was more complicated due to the fact that the island was totally isolated and difficult to get to at the moment since the bridge had been washed out.

Gracie remembered hearing some guys at the station talking about how two people on the island were doing what might be considered an Uber service. One man—Stan—drove people around here, and another—Mel—provided a water taxi back and forth to the mainland.

If Gracie could meet up with them, she could get off this island. But since she had no phone and limited money . . . it would be tricky.

She hoped to borrow some money from Dillon. She'd pay him back as soon as she could.

But that didn't stop the guilt from pounding at her.

Gracie rinsed her mouth and continued to think everything through.

When she got to the mainland, she would borrow Dillon's old car. He'd said he kept a set of keys here at the cottage, and Gracie thought she could find them. There were a lot of holes in her plan. But she hoped to figure out a way around them.

After she got the car, she wasn't exactly sure where she would go. She'd thought about Florida. Maybe one of the bigger cities down there, where she could just blend in among the crowds.

Another part of her felt a surprising surge of sadness at the thought of leaving this windswept place.

How was it possible that Gracie had grown to love this island so quickly?

Part of her would actually miss Dillon.

Dillon.

Even the thought of him made grief clutch her heart. The emotion didn't make sense. The two of them drove each other crazy. Yet she'd be lying if she didn't admit they did have some type of bond.

You can come back here again one day, she reminded herself. This doesn't have to be permanent.

Gracie didn't have to sacrifice her character in order to survive. This was just a temporary arrangement. Once things with Constantine were behind her, she could figure out the rest of this mess she'd created.

She wiped her mouth and opened the door, ready to emerge and get ready for her great escape.

She would still follow through on her promise to Dillon. As soon as she took over the reins at the company, she'd do everything she could to make sure that the wild horses here on this island were highlighted as well as the importance of their safety.

For now, she just needed to wait for the others to leave the house.

Then she would set her plan into action.

DILLON SENSED that Gracie was acting strange all morning—during breakfast and even as she'd gotten ready.

He knew it probably had to do with Philip's disappearance.

But his gut told him there was more to her shifting gaze than that.

When his mom had mentioned she was going out of town, Gracie's eyes had lit up with excitement.

She was planning something.

Planning to leave, wasn't she?

A twist of anger tugged in his gut. Gracie had promised him that she would stay. So why was she ready to run now?

Dillon would do everything in his power not to let that happen.

As soon as he kissed his mom's cheek goodbye and she left with Emmy, Dillon turned to Gracie as she absently straightened the living room.

"I can't leave you here alone today," he started. "You can come to work with me."

Her eyes widened with surprise. "Go to work

with you? Why would I do that? I'll just stay here and lock the doors."

"Now that Philip is missing, the whole situation is even more precarious. I don't think it's a good idea that you stay here by yourself."

"But . . ." She opened her mouth and shut it again.

His announcement had thrown her for a loop, hadn't it?

Good.

"Gracie." Dillon stepped closer and lowered his voice. "I promised to protect you. That's what I'm going to do."

"But . . ." Her words trailed again. It was almost as if she looked for an excuse but couldn't come up with any. Finally, she said, "I don't want to be in your way."

"You won't be. I'll make sure of that." He winked.

She frowned but finally nodded.

Satisfaction washed over Dillon.

He'd just bought himself some time.

But this was far from being over.

Just as the thought went through his head, someone knocked at the door.

He assumed his mom and Emmy had come back because they'd forgotten something. Still, Dillon was on guard as he strode toward the front of the house.

But when he threw the door open, the person standing on the other side made him reach for his gun.

CHAPTER THIRTY-THREE

"CONSTANTINE?" Gracie gasped and stepped back.

As she did, Dillon wedged himself in front of her, blocking her from the man at the door.

Constantine strode inside, anger beaming from his eyes as he turned to Dillon. "You! You said you hadn't seen her."

Dillon's shoulders and chest seemed to expand at the man's words. "You're not going to come into my house and make demands of me."

Constantine's nostrils flared. "As an official on this island, I'd think you'd be obligated to tell the truth."

Gracie sensed the tension rising between the men and stepped forward. "What are you doing here, Constantine?"

His eyes narrowed as he glowered at her. "I'm looking for you, of course. I've been worried, especially after that note was found with your dress. I'm sure you heard about it on the news."

She was certain that he'd been the one who'd planted those things. She wasn't going to buy into his game. "How did you even find me?"

"I asked around on the island. Talked to the man whose boat you stole. I put things together, and that led me here."

She raised her chin. "I'm not going back with you."

Constantine leveled his voice. "Gracie, you need help."

Anger surged through her. She knew exactly what he was doing—trying to make her look weak. "The only reason I need help is to get away from you."

His eyes flickered with anger. "You're not in your right state of mind. Everyone has noticed lately."

Gracie's hands fisted at her sides. "You don't know what you're talking about."

"I'm here to bring you home. I have a therapist you can talk to—"

"I'm not going anywhere with you!"

CAPE CORRAL KEEPER   235

Constantine sighed and glanced at Dillon. "Do you mind giving me a minute alone with my fiancée?"

"I do." Dillon's steely gaze went to Constantine's. "Because she's not your fiancée. She's my wife."

DILLON WATCHED as the man's face turned a darker shade of red.

"What are you talking about?" Constantine demanded, disbelief stretching through his voice.

Dillon stepped closer to Gracie and wrapped his arm around her shoulders. As he did, Gracie slipped her arm around his waist. Together, they were the picture of a happy couple.

"That's right." Gracie raised her chin, that familiar stubbornness returning to her gaze. "Dillon and I are married."

Constantine's eyes narrowed. "We were supposed to get married only a couple of days ago. How did this happen?"

Gracie shrugged, still appearing unaffected by the man. "When it's right it's right."

Constantine's gaze shifted to Dillon.

Dillon said nothing but kept his eyes hard as he stared back at the man.

"I can't believe this." Constantine shook his head as if in disbelief, an almost airy chuckle escaping. "Something smells fishy."

"Well, you can believe it," Gracie said. "I'm here, and I'm at home now. There's no turning back."

Constantine's feet remained planted, as if he was unable to remove himself from the house.

Finally, his gaze went back to Dillon's. Something hardened there, showing a shift in thought. "I'm getting my lawyer."

"Why would you get a lawyer, Constantine?" Gracie asked. "What good would that possibly do?"

"This guy is obviously taking advantage of someone who's been through a severe emotional trauma." Satisfaction gleamed in the man's eyes.

Gracie fisted her hands. "The only trauma in my life was you!"

Constantine shook his head, almost as if he pitied Gracie. "You have a long history of being unstable. I've documented all of it. Once I show a judge all the facts, your new 'marriage' is going to be null and void. You just wait. This isn't the last you have seen of me. Not by any stretch of the imagination."

With that, Constantine stormed outside, slamming the door behind him.

Dillon turned toward Gracie, trying to take inventory of how she was doing.

Her eyes looked wide and frightened, but otherwise she seemed to be holding herself together.

He rubbed her arms, knowing that had to be difficult for her to hear.

"What are you thinking?" he asked.

She shook her head and squeezed the skin between her eyes. "Marrying you isn't going to get me out of anything, is it? Constantine is just going to keep coming after me until he gets his way."

"I don't see how that's possible."

"He said he's going to hire a lawyer and take this before a judge. What if this judge thinks that Constantine is right?"

Dillon rubbed his jaw. "Why would anyone in their right mind think Constantine was right?"

"Constantine is very convincing—he'll think of something. My guess is that he wants to make me look crazy, and then, once we're married, he's going to be able to take over all the affairs of my estate."

"Is there anything in particular that may look bad for you? I need to know, Gracie."

She let out a sigh and a memory seemed to pass through her gaze.

As Gracie turned toward him, Dillon braced himself for whatever she had to say.

CHAPTER THIRTY-FOUR

"THERE IS ONE THING." Gracie felt sick to her stomach. This was the last thing she wanted to talk about with Dillon.

"You can tell me, Gracie." Dillon's voice sounded so sincere, so soothing as they stood in front of each other, Constantine's ghost still lingering in the room.

Would Dillon change how he felt about her when Gracie told him about the . . . about the incident, for lack of a better word?

She rubbed her hands on her jeans and nodded. It wasn't like she was trying to impress the man or something. Besides, he'd done so much for her. She couldn't withhold things.

"About a month ago, White Star Media had their

annual company party. Constantine went with me—this was right when we'd started having problems. He got me something to drink when we got there. After I took a few sips, I don't . . . well, I don't really remember much about the rest of the evening."

Dillon's eyes narrowed. "What do you mean?"

She drew in a long shaky breath. "I think he put something in my drink."

"Do you remember anything that happened afterward?" Concern rang through his voice.

"I only know what I heard." Gracie's cheeks heated at the memory. "I had a couple of people call me afterward and say that I wasn't acting like myself that night. I was . . ."

Dillon leaned closer. "You were what?"

She swallowed hard. "Apparently, I was dancing on the tables and being overall obnoxious, almost like I was drunk. But I didn't have any alcohol. There were some pictures taken. I don't even look like myself in them."

"Why would Constantine do that to you?"

"To make me look incompetent. It's the only thing that makes sense. I still get embarrassed when I think about it." She felt her cheeks heating even as she relayed the incident.

"Certainly, those who know you—really know you—knew something was wrong."

"I'd like to think that. But other times, I have to wonder how many people really know me at all." Gracie clamped her mouth shut. She hadn't meant to say that much. The fear wasn't something she often—or ever—shared with people. Something about it brought her an unusual measure of shame.

"Did you report the incident to anyone?"

She shook her head. "How could I? I had no proof. Besides, this was after I'd already realized the truth about Constantine. He was manipulating me, even at that point. He wanted to force me to marry him."

"He sounds like a very calculating man."

"He is."

"Did you confront him about the drink?"

"I did. He denied it. Of course. But I know the truth. Who else would have done something that horrible?"

Her question rang through the air.

DILLON HAD UNDERESTIMATED the lengths that this Constantine guy would go to. It wasn't enough for him to ruin Gracie's life, but he also wanted to take over her parents' company and to destroy her character.

Anger roiled through Dillon at the thought. How could someone sink this low and still live with themselves?

Yet he had dealt with plenty of people who did things like that. They only thought about one person —and that was themselves.

Dillon wished there was some way he could comfort her. He sensed Gracie was on the verge of falling apart. He could see it in the quiver of her chin, in the deep breaths she drew in.

As soon as he had a moment alone, he would call Grant and Dash.

He needed to figure out where Constantine was staying on the island.

Then Dillon would personally make sure that someone kept an eye on him at all times. He couldn't allow the man to cause any more trouble for Gracie.

Dillon started to reach for her, to try to find the right words.

But before he could, his phone rang. There was an emergency he needed to get to.

But there was no way he was leaving Gracie here by herself.

She was going to have to come with him, and he wouldn't take no for an answer.

CHAPTER THIRTY-FIVE

GRACIE SAT in Dillon's truck and watched as Dillon and Colby disappeared inside a two-story cottage on the south end of the island.

From what she understood, a man had called 911 with symptoms of a heart attack before the line went dead. Dillon and Colby, who were also EMTs, had rushed to help him.

As promised, Gracie sat in Dillon's truck with the windows up and doors locked. She'd scooted low so no one could spot her.

She hoped that the man inside the house would be okay.

While waiting, Gracie glanced out the window and spotted three of the island's wild horses in the distance. The creatures were gorgeous. She could see why Dillon loved this area so much. What was there not to like? Between the ocean, the close-knit community, and the wild horses, this was a place dreams were made of.

Gracie glanced at her watch. The two men had gone inside ten minutes ago. She knew situations like this could take time, but she'd expected Dillon and Colby to emerge by now.

She glanced at the blue, two-story house with its interesting angles and more modern design. It didn't necessarily fit with the other houses here on the island. It was missing the warmth of the usual cottages, with their eaves and shutters and cedar siding.

As she studied the house, she squinted.

Was that someone moving at the back of the property?

It was.

Gracie froze as she spotted a man dressed in all black running from the back of the house and into the woods behind it.

What was going on?

She didn't know.

But whatever it was, it looked like trouble.

"HELLO?" Dillon called again.

But there was no answer.

He and Colby headed to the last bedroom down the second-floor hallway.

It was the only room they hadn't checked yet.

Gear in hand, they stepped inside the dark space. It looked like the hurricane shutters had been pulled down outside, and the room stretched around in an L shape. An old, stained beige couch and some assorted tables scattered across the brown shag carpet.

As they stepped around the corner, Dillon fully expected to see someone lying on the floor, needing their help.

But the place was empty.

"I don't see anyone here, Boss." Colby looked over at him and shrugged.

The muscles on Dillon's back knit together even more tightly. "I don't either. I don't know what's going on here."

"Maybe the person who called managed to get out of the house before we arrived," Colby suggested. "Or maybe a neighbor took him to the clinic."

"Maybe." It was a possibility. But Dillon didn't think so.

As they turned to go back, the door to the room slammed.

Alarm shot through Dillon.

He rushed toward it and jerked on the handle.

The door didn't budge.

Had someone locked them in?

Dillon threw his weight into it, but the door still didn't move. It was almost like someone had barricaded it.

"Boss?" Colby looked at him.

Dillon's jaw hardened. "Someone locked us in here for some reason."

"Why would they do that?"

"That's the question I'm asking myself also."

Just as the words left his lips, Dillon spotted a small tube coming in through an air vent on the floor.

He rushed toward it and examined the tube a moment before realization dawned on him.

"There's gas coming into the room." Dillon locked his gaze on Colby, knowing he had to drive home his point. "If we don't get out of here soon, we're both going to sleep for a very long time."

CHAPTER THIRTY-SIX

GRACIE FORGOT her promise to Dillon. Instead, she rushed up the steps to the cottage.

She had to figure out what was going on.

Her gut told her Dillon's life depended on it.

She twisted the handle on the front door, but it was locked.

Had the guys locked it behind them?

Or had the person Gracie spotted darting from the house done this to ensure no one could get inside to help Dillon and Colby in an emergency?

Panic surged through her at the thought.

She had to figure out a way to get inside.

She darted to the other side of the deck.

No other doors were on this side.

She tried the windows.

They were locked.

Think, Gracie. Think!

Gripping the rough wood railing, she peered over the deck, trying to get a glimpse of the other side of the house.

She squinted.

Why had the hurricane shutters been drawn on upstairs windows at the back of the house?

It didn't matter, Gracie supposed. The house was on stilts. She couldn't reach those windows anyway. Even if she could find a ladder—the key word being *if*—it would take too much time to get to the windows and figure out the metal shutters.

There had to be something else she could do.

That man had escaped out the back, she remembered. There had to be another door back there somewhere.

Gracie rushed down the steps and around the house.

Another stairway led to the back of the house. But it was just as she suspected—the door there was locked also.

What was she going to do?

She glanced around.

She had to think of something—and soon.

DILLON HADN'T BROUGHT any of his firefighting equipment up with him. He'd come expecting a medical emergency.

Not this.

That was exactly what the person who'd called had planned on.

"What do we do?" Colby turned toward him, waiting for Dillon to call the shots.

Dillon glanced around. "Let's try the windows again. Maybe we can shove the shutters open from inside."

Colby nodded but touched his temple as he rushed across the room. "I'm feeling lightheaded."

"Stay with me, Colby."

"You know it, Boss."

Colby was tough. Still a little green when it came to being a firefighter. But Dillon had depended on him on more than one occasion, and Colby had never let him down.

They examined each of the three wood-framed windows. It was no use. The shutters were each latched in place and unmovable.

Dillon had already tried to pull the tube out from the air vent. It didn't budge. When he pushed it, it simply dropped deeper into the vent until it was unreachable.

If he had to guess, the man who'd lured them here had bought a cannister of carbon monoxide. He'd probably put it in the utility closet near the air handler.

He'd meticulously planned this.

Dillon didn't know how much longer he and Colby had. Slipping into an unconscious state would happen gradually, so he and Colby would probably hardly realize it.

That made this situation even more dangerous.

Someone had orchestrated this.

Had wanted to see them hurt.

Or die.

Dillon pushed on the shutters harder, one more time.

It was no use. They were solid.

Dillon needed an ax to get out of here.

But they didn't have one.

He glanced at the door again.

He would ram into it and break his shoulder if that's what it took to get out of here.

Because they didn't have much time.

CHAPTER THIRTY-SEVEN

AS GRACIE RAN BACK around the house, she searched for something to break the glass in one of the windows.

She wished she could dial 911, but it might be too late by the time they got here anyway. Besides—Dillon and Colby *were* 911. But maybe there were other guys on duty. She didn't know enough about the area yet to say for certain.

She only knew she had to help Dillon and Colby.

The only thing on the deck was a small metal chair.

It would have to work.

Picking up the chair, she held it over her shoulder. Using all her energy, she slammed it into the window by the door.

The glass shattered.

She breathed a little easier—but only for a moment.

Wasting no time, she pulled off the flannel shirt she wore over her white T-shirt and wrapped it around her arm.

Gracie brushed away the sharp shards of glass still left around the frame.

As she did, something sliced into her skin.

She gasped.

As Gracie pulled her arm back, blood appeared.

The glass had slashed through her shirt.

No!

Everything spun around her—but only for a minute. Blood always had that effect on her.

Gracie had to pull herself together.

Dillon's and Colby's lives depended on it, she reminded herself again.

She pulled in a breath before climbing through the window. Glass crunched beneath her feet as she landed on the other side.

She scanned the room around her. This was the living room, and the interior was just as sleek and modern as the outside. That meant everything was streamlined with not a lot of extra furniture.

It made it easy to search the space.

No sign of Dillon and Colby yet.

"Dillon?" she called.

Nothing.

She darted toward the back of the house, glancing in each room as she passed.

Nothing.

She charged toward the second level and did the same.

Nothing.

But the door at the end of the hallway was closed—and a table had been shoved in front of it.

"Dillon?" she called.

A moment later, she heard, "Gracie?"

He was there!

"I'm coming!" she yelled.

Now she just had to figure out a way to get him out.

As Gracie glanced around, she pressed her shirt harder into her arm.

Her cut throbbed.

The blood was seeping through the fabric surrounding it.

But she'd deal with that later.

"I'm going to get you out!" Gracie yelled.

"Someone is funneling some kind of gas into the

room," Dillon yelled. "Be careful, Gracie! Whoever did this could still be out there."

She shuddered and turned around, halfway expecting to see someone watching her from the other end of the hallway.

But that man she'd seen outside the house was long gone.

Gracie had seen him skulk away.

She grabbed the table and tugged it. The furniture was heavier than she'd imagined, and the hallway made it difficult for her to manage—not to mention her injured arm.

But she could do it. She knew she could.

"Gracie?" Dillon's voice stretched through the air.

She tugged the table again, her teeth grinding together in determination.

"I've almost got it," she told him.

"We don't have much time."

Gracie gave the table another tug. It moved enough for her to reach the handle. She twisted the lock and pulled the door open.

As she did, Dillon and Colby stumbled out.

They drank in deep gulps of air as they leaned over the table.

Concern ricocheted through Gracie.

Thank goodness she'd been here.

It was clear neither of them would have lasted long in there.

AS DILLON INHALED another breath of air, he glanced at Gracie. His gaze went to the shirt wrapped around her arm.

She was bleeding.

A lot.

In fact, droplets hit the floor beneath her.

He reached for her, forgetting his own issues. "What happened?"

"Oh, this?" But as she glanced down at her wound, her eyelids drooped as if she might pass out. "I had to break a window to get in, and I cut myself on some glass."

"We need to put some pressure on that. You're losing a lot of blood."

"I'll be fine," she murmured.

Dillon wasn't so sure about that.

Just then, he heard someone yell downstairs. "Dillon? Colby?"

Grant.

Backup had arrived, and just in time.

"Colby, you tell him what happened." Dillon

held Gracie's arm, trying to keep it raised. "I'm going to take Gracie to the clinic. She needs to have this stitched up."

"Stitches?" Her voice sounded weak, like she was losing it. "I hate needles. I'll be fine."

Dillon pulled the shirt from around her arm back and saw the deep cut. "You don't have much choice here, sweetheart. But I'll be there with you. I promise."

Before he could try any more to convince her, she started to sink to the floor.

Dillon caught her before she totally collapsed.

He'd carry her to the clinic if he had to.

This woman had just saved his life.

CHAPTER THIRTY-EIGHT

GRACIE PULLED her eyes open and gasped.

Where was she?

She pushed herself upright as panic flooded her.

Had Constantine gotten her? Had he taken her somewhere she'd never escape?

A cry lodged in her throat.

"Gracie? It's okay. I'm here."

As she blinked, Dillon's face came into view hovering over her. Everything else blurred except for his features.

Until today's events rushed back to her.

The house.

Seeing the man outside.

Finding Dillon and Colby in a gas-filled room.

If she'd just been a few minutes later, they could have . . .

Another cry caught in her throat.

That had been too close.

"What . . . happened?" She squinted and glanced around as her vision cleared.

She was at a medical facility of some sort, but she couldn't remember how she got there.

"You passed out," Dillon told her. "Maybe it was when you saw the blood from your cut."

The blood? Gracie glanced at her arm and saw the bandage there.

That was right. She had cut herself on the broken window.

"You had to get seven stitches," Dillon explained.

"Seven?" She hadn't realized the cut was that big.

He nodded. "You lost quite a bit of blood."

She rubbed the bandage, fighting the wooziness that tried to come again. "I guess I did."

Someone else stepped into the room with a clipboard in hand. "You're awake. That's great news. I'm Dr. Knightly."

She glanced at the man. He certainly didn't look like any doctor she'd ever met. He looked more like a surfer wearing a lab coat and stethoscope.

CAPE CORRAL KEEPER   261

Dillon didn't seem to doubt the man, so he must be legit.

"How are you feeling?" Dr. Knightly asked.

Gracie shook her head, trying to figure out how to answer that question. "I guess I'm fine."

"I'm glad to hear that. We stitched you up, and you should be good to go. The cut was pretty deep, so we also gave you some pain medication."

"Pain medication?" Alarm raced through her.

"You were in a lot of pain, and we asked you if you wanted some," the doctor said. "You said you did."

"I don't remember any of that. I must have really been out of it." She swallowed hard. "What kind?"

"Percocet."

She groaned, dread filling her. "I should warn you—that stuff . . . most pain killers, for that matter . . . they make me act a little crazy."

"Crazy?" Dillon raised his eyebrows.

"That's what I've been told. Don't worry. I should be fine. It's just what my college roommates told me. I had to take it when I broke an arm after rollerblading down a hill. What about you? Are you okay?"

"I'm sure I'll be fine," Dillon said. "It's you I'm worried about. You ready to get back to the house?"

She nodded. "Yes, I'm more than ready."

Dillon helped her from the bed and slipped an arm around her.

Thank God, he'd been there to help her.

She'd only known him a few days, and he'd already proven to be invaluable.

DILLON AND GRACIE were almost at his cottage. But with every rotation of the tires, Gracie was becoming more and more loopy.

She was correct when she'd said pain medicine made her crazy. Not in an insane kind of way but in a funny, almost inebriated manner.

For the entire ride home, she'd rambled on and on about how much she loved the color pink, how horses were the coolest creatures to ever roam the earth, and how everyone should be required to watch at least one cat video per day.

Dillon had mostly listened.

But really, his mind was on the events of the day.

He didn't know what might have happened if Gracie hadn't shown up when she did.

The situation back at the house had been close.

He'd already talked to Grant and Dash and had

given his statement. They were examining the house for any fingerprints or other clues that may have been left as well as searching the island for their suspect.

Someone had tried to kill Dillon and Colby.

Most likely, that person was Constantine.

If Dillon was dead, then the man would be free to marry Gracie.

It was the only motive that made sense.

Dillon's gut tightened at the realization.

As they pulled up to Dillon's house—their house, he should say—he put the truck in Park and turned toward Gracie.

"Are we home?" Her words sounded perky and slightly slurred.

"We are."

"You have a cute house," she told him, resting her head back on the seat and staring at him with a cozy look in her eyes. "You really do. I like it."

He smiled, despite her out-of-it state. "I'm glad."

"To be honest, I didn't think I'd like it here in Cape Corral," she continued. "But I do. I feel like I can breathe, you know? Maybe it's the fresh air. Maybe it's something else. I really don't know."

"Maybe."

"You know, I was worried about you today." Her

voice turned serious, and she straightened. "I don't want anything to happen to you, especially not because of me."

"It wasn't your fault, Gracie."

She reached for him and squeezed his forearm. "It feels like my fault. Everything feels like my fault."

"Don't worry about it, Gracie. You just worry about getting better."

She nodded, her eyes drooping again.

The next thing he knew, Gracie leaned against his shoulder, her arms circling his bicep and hugging it.

"I don't know what to do, Dillon." Her words slurred.

"What do you mean?"

"I just don't know what to do," she repeated, her voice fading.

"Everything is going to be okay, Gracie." Dillon slipped his arm from her hold and placed it around her shoulder instead, pulling her closer.

To his surprise, she cuddled up next to him, seeming to relax in his embrace.

He held her, in no hurry to move. Her warmth felt good next to him. The moment . . . it almost seemed normal.

"Dillon?" she whispered.

"Yes?"

"I feel safe when I'm with you. Thank you."

Against his better instincts, Dillon gently pressed a kiss on the top of her head. "I'm glad."

"I haven't felt safe since . . . since my parents died."

His heart pounded with empathy. Gracie had never been this raw or vulnerable before. Dillon knew it was most likely the drug talking. But it was good to see her let down her guard.

"You're not all that bad, Gracie McGrath," he murmured. "Do you know that?"

She said nothing, and Dillon wondered if he'd blown it. Maybe he should have kept his mouth shut.

Then Dillon heard her softly breathing.

She was asleep, wasn't she?

Dillon let out a quiet chuckle.

What a day.

CHAPTER THIRTY-NINE

I KNOW where you are now, and I'm coming for you. No one will get in my way. Not even Dillon McGrath.

He may be strong, but I'm smart.

I will win.

I have a plan that you'll never see coming.

He stared at the house.

Dillon's house.

Gracie's house.

They'd gotten married?

It was almost laughable. If it wasn't so desperate, he might keel over in a belly-aching laugh.

Then again, maybe it shouldn't be a surprise. Desperate people did desperate things.

Gracie still wouldn't win.

He wouldn't let her.

In fact, he had a new plan that he'd set into motion tomorrow.

A smile curled his lips at the thought.

He stood in the shadows, staring at the house where Gracie was now staying. As he did, more bitterness and vengeance brewed in his gut like a deadly potion in a cauldron.

This was no longer about getting what he wanted.

This was about teaching a lesson.

To both Gracie and Dillon.

He would enjoy every minute of it.

Because she'd brought this upon herself.

CHAPTER FORTY

GRACIE SAT up in bed the next morning and blinked.

She hardly remembered coming into her room last night.

For that matter, she *didn't* remember coming into her room last night.

How had she gotten here?

A sickly feeling loomed in her gut as she realized she couldn't remember.

The door opened, and Dillon stepped into the room. "Good, you're awake. How are you feeling?"

"I'm . . . okay, I guess." Gracie glanced at her arm. That was right. She'd cut herself on the window. Dillon had taken her to the clinic.

A few hazy details teased the edge of her thoughts.

"I brought you some coffee." He set a cup on the table beside her. "Just like you like it."

"Thank you."

"Can I bring you anything else?" Dillon studied her face, as if trying to determine her mindset.

"I . . . don't think so. But you can tell me what happened last night? I don't remember coming here."

His hands went to his hips as he stood between the bed and the mat on the floor where he'd slept. "I had to carry you to bed. You were out."

"They gave me pain medication at the clinic." She groaned as more memories flooded her. "I didn't do anything stupid, did I?"

Dillon stared at her another moment before finally shaking his head. "Nothing stupid at all."

"That's a relief." Thank goodness.

He sat down on the other end of the bed. "Look, I forgot to mention it to you, but there's a reception tonight for my friends Levi and Dani. They just got back from their honeymoon. They didn't have a big ceremony before they left, so they're going to celebrate now. I'd love for you to go with me."

"Are you sure it's safe?"

"Constantine already knows where you live. He'd have to be mighty brave to show up there."

"True."

"Besides, I'll keep my eyes on you, and all my friends will be there. It would be hard for Constantine to pull any stunts in a crowd like that."

After a moment, Gracie nodded. "Okay then. If you think it's safe."

It actually sounded fun and halfway normal—two things Gracie would welcome.

Dillon smiled and stood. "Oh, and one more thing. My mom is leaving today. She's going to visit some friends up in Virginia, but she'll be back for Thanksgiving in a few weeks. After you drink your coffee, she'd love to say goodbye."

"Of course." Gracie wouldn't let Marla leave without a hug.

With another nod, Dillon left.

He seemed . . . different, Gracie realized. But why?

She rubbed her hand across her cheek.

She really hoped she hadn't done anything stupid last night.

But why did she have a feeling she had?

THIRTY MINUTES LATER, Dillon's mom stepped toward the door with her bag in hand. Colby was going to give her a ride to the boat taxi that would take her to the mainland. She'd left her car there when she came to visit.

Gracie had already given her a hug goodbye.

Now it was Dillon's turn.

He pulled his mom into a long embrace. "I'm so glad you came."

"I'm glad I could be here." She leaned closer and lowered her voice. "I really like Gracie, Dillon."

Dillon glanced over his mom's shoulder at Gracie. She stood in the kitchen but looked away, as if giving them some privacy. "I'm glad you like her."

His mom pulled out of the hug but still remained close. "It's good to see you happy again."

Dillon started to repeat what she'd said, unsure if he'd heard correctly . . . but he caught himself before he did.

Thankfully.

His mom was so close to seeing through him already.

"It's . . . it's good to be happy again," he finally said.

His mom grinned and patted his face.

But as his mom waved goodbye to Gracie one more time, Dillon lingered on her words.

Did he really look happy? With Gracie?

Maybe his mom had seen something he couldn't.

Or maybe his mom was seeing what she wanted to see.

That last option made the most sense.

CHAPTER FORTY-ONE

AS GRACIE WATCHED Dillon hug his mom good-bye, surprising warmth filled her chest.

She'd always loved a man who loved his mama.

Maybe *loved* was a strong word. But still, the scene was touching.

Gracie was going to miss Marla. She'd truly enjoyed getting to know the woman. At least, Gracie would see her again in a few weeks.

Until then, there was something else Gracie wanted to do. She'd been thinking about it all morning. She hoped Dillon might be on board with her idea. She knew he had the day off work.

As soon as the door closed and Colby pulled away with Marla, Gracie turned to Dillon.

"If you don't have anything to do, how would you

feel about taking me to see the wild horses?" she asked.

Dillon did a double take at her as he leaned against the door with his thick arms crossed over his chest. "Really?"

She shrugged. "If I'm going to make sure that there's a piece done on them for White Star Media, I need to know what I'm pitching."

Dillon stared at her a moment before nodding. "That makes sense. How would you feel about seeing them via horseback?"

"I think that sounds awesome. Do you think I'll be okay with this?" She raised her arm, displayed her bandage.

"It doesn't hurt to move your hand, does it?"

She shook her head.

"Then you should be fine."

She grinned. "Good."

"Okay then." Dillon straightened, still looking surprised at her suggestion. "I'll go get two horses saddled up."

A few minutes later, they were at the stable. As Dillon worked inside, Gracie lingered near the doorway, staring out at the sandy landscape in the distance.

Part of her felt as if she'd been swept into a

whole new world. The windswept scenery was one thing, among many, that made this place so fascinating.

As she waited there, a truck pulled to a stop in front of her.

Instantly, her muscles tensed.

This wasn't the truck she'd seen Constantine in. It was too new, too nice.

But still, Gracie didn't want anyone other than those who were absolutely necessary to see her here.

A man who appeared to be around her age lowered his window and leaned out, leering at her. "Never seen you around here before."

He seemed more like the kind of guy Gracie would have encountered up in DC than here in Cape Corral. There was something too finessed and cultured about him for him to be a saltwater cowboy.

She said nothing, just stared at him, hoping he'd go away.

"If you need anyone to show you around the island, you just let me know. I can show you all kinds of things." A smug grin appeared on his face.

Gracie raised her chin, hating those kind of lines. "I'm doing fine by myself, thank you."

"You think you're doing fine . . . but you don't

know fine until you've spent some time with me." He winked.

Just then, Dillon appeared beside her and wrapped his arm around her waist. His voice turned steely as he addressed the man. "You need to stay away from my wife."

The man's eyebrows shot in the air. "Your wife? My apologies. You did good for yourself, Dillon McGrath."

Gracie glanced at Dillon and saw his eyes were narrow, his jaw tight. He really didn't like this guy, did he?

Neither said anything else until finally the man in the truck waved. "See you around."

The truck pulled away.

Just who was that man?

And why did he get under Dillon's skin so quickly?

DILLON WAS grateful that Gracie didn't ask too many questions about the earlier confrontation.

Instead, the two of them trotted on their horses beside each other down the sandy stretch of land.

They'd cut over the dunes and now strolled by the ocean.

Dillon would never get tired of this sight—the open expanse of sand, bordered by the crashing waves. Sometimes the water looked turquoise, and other times it appeared stormy gray. However it looked, the sight was enough to take Dillon's breath away.

Gracie seemed equally entranced by it.

He was glad she was distracted. Dillon's friends were still trying to track down where Constantine was staying. It was better if Gracie didn't know that, that she didn't get her hopes up.

"Who was that man?" Gracie finally asked.

"That was Johnny Ferguson."

Her eyebrows shot up. "Of the notorious Ferguson clan?"

"The one and only."

"He seems like a piece of work."

"He is," Dillon said. "He and his family think they own this island. They act entitled, for that matter."

"I'm sorry to hear that," Gracie murmured.

"The thing is, the people here on this island . . . they're resilient. Some of the families go back for generations. They can trace their lineages back to old sea captains and a few people even to pirates. The locals have battled storms, erosion, flooding, and blistering hot summers. Through it all, they've proven they're survivors."

Gracie glanced at him and smiled. "They sound like my kind of people."

"The Fergusons have been orchestrating the campaign to build a resort here," Dillon continued. "They hired someone to come around and hand out signs for people to put in their lawns. But you know what? Not one person has given in and done it."

"I think that says a lot for your community and how strong it is," Gracie said.

Dillon nodded. "So do I. It shows that we're stronger than anything that's thrown at us, whether we were born and raised here or if we're someone who moved here because we fell in love with the island."

"You guys are going to win this one," Gracie said. "I can feel it. People used to call it the Loveland intuition. My dad had it, and people say that's why his business was so successful."

"Is that right?"

She nodded. "You just wait and see. I'm going to be right on this one."

He glanced over at Gracie as her blonde hair blew in the wind.

She'd borrowed one of Dillon's cowboy hats, and she was a sight to behold in it, especially with her flannel shirt and jeans.

She seemed to fit here on Cape Corral.

Which wouldn't have seemed possible a few days ago when Dillon rescued her from the Currituck Sound.

It was amazing how time could change a person's perspective—oftentimes for the best.

"Did you guys happen to check into my suggestion of looking for any endangered animals on the land where they want to build?" Gracie asked.

Dillon welcomed the change of subject. It was better than thinking about how gorgeous his wife was—his wife with whom he shared a platonic relationship.

"As a matter of fact, we're having someone look into that now," Dillon finally said. "It was a good idea. Thanks for the suggestion."

"No problem. I hope you're able to make some headway and stop this family from doing any harm to this island."

"Me too."

Gracie pointed to something in the distance. "Hey, isn't that Rocky?"

Dillon glanced over and saw the lone stallion munching on some sea oats. "It sure is."

"Would you look at that? He's not alone after all."

Dillon watched as a cattle egret sat on Rocky's back and hitched a ride down the shoreline.

Maybe a lone stallion didn't have to be alone. Maybe all it took was a different perspective. Maybe being part of a relationship didn't always look the way someone thought it would.

Dillon glanced at Gracie and saw a smile stretch across her face as she watched the horse.

Why did seeing her happy bring Dillon so much delight?

Things weren't supposed to happen this way.

So why were they?

CHAPTER FORTY-TWO

GRACIE AND DILLON had returned to his place after three hours of exploring the island by horseback.

She'd loved every minute of the experience—even riding a horse.

She'd done so a few times as a child, but it was different here. She'd been on a mare named Sage—a beautiful chestnut mustang. The breeze had been perfect, the sun had been out, and Dillon had been good company.

He'd even taken her to a place called The Screen Porch Café for a quick bite to eat. The home-cooked crab cake sandwich had been delicious and had left her wanting more. Plus, the family-like atmosphere of the restaurant reminded her of a place she'd seen only in movies or in books. There was a real sense of belonging among the residents here.

For a moment, Gracie had felt like she was a part of life here on the island.

It was a good feeling.

Gracie snapped back to the present. She'd changed into a blue knit dress, jean jacket, and some borrowed cowboy boots for Dillon's friends' wedding reception.

Dillon had brought her to a beautiful barn located on the edge of the Currituck Sound. The building was surrounded by nothing except a gazebo and a few solitary live oak trees whose silhouettes added drama to the shoreline.

A crowd of probably fifty people had gathered, just in time to see the sun set over the water.

Right now, Gracie leaned against one of the wood posts inside the barn, crossed her arms, and watched as Dillon mingled with the people at the reception. He seemed so in his element here—and not like the brute she'd first assumed him to be.

Today had been really nice—so nice she'd almost forgotten her problems.

"He's a good man," someone said beside her.

She looked up and saw Dash Fulton standing there.

She instantly liked the man. He seemed nice, personable, and humble each time they'd spoken.

"He *is* a good man," Gracie said.

"We like to call him Lasso Man around here," Dash continued. "He's always won the contest the guys and I have, but I'm determined to take that title away from him."

She smiled. "Good luck with that."

Dash's smile disappeared. "You know, Dillon pitched in every weekend for the past four months to help Smith build this barn. They call it Smith's Hope."

Her eyebrows shot up as she looked around. The high ceiling had wood arches and beams. The workmanship looked top-notch, and the space was clearly more of a meeting area than a working barn.

"It's beautiful," she finally muttered. "It really is."

"Smith's other barn was struck by lightning. Dillon and Colby helped put the fire out, but they saw how the loss devastated Smith—the man had a string of bad luck. That's when Dillon stepped in to help. He's the kind of guy who always thinks of others."

Gracie's throat tightened. That was why Dillon had married her, wasn't it? To help her out?

Again, it was an example of how selfless he could be.

Dash had possibly been trying to make her feel better.

But something about his words made Gracie realize everything Dillon had given up in order to help her.

How could she ever make it up to him?

DILLON LOOKED up as someone tapped him on the shoulder. When he turned, he saw Mrs. Minnie standing there. The seventy-something owned The Screen Porch Café and was a fixture here around town.

"How about a dance, stranger?"

He grinned. "I would love to dance. But are you sure Mark won't mind?"

Mark was her husband.

"Are you kidding? Mark's hips are so bad that the closest he comes to dancing is trying to sweep the broom across the wood floor. He's a sight to see when he does that, believe you me."

Dillon fought a grin and put his arms on Mrs. Minnie's waist. She wasn't shy about putting her hands on his shoulders, but she didn't step too close.

As they began to sway under the string lights, Dillon glanced across the room and saw Gracie and Dash talking.

The sight of her caused a surprising warmth to rush through him.

How was it possible that Dillon's feelings for the woman were growing? He asked himself that every day, it seemed.

This was supposed to be a business arrangement. But somehow, it felt like it was turning into much more.

"Did I hear you got yourself married?" Mrs. Minnie asked as Lonestar's "Amazed" played overhead.

"I did."

"Who's the lucky girl?"

Dillon nodded across the barn. "Her name is Gracie."

Mrs. Minnie followed his gaze. "She's a pretty thing."

"She's sweet too."

"That's good. I always wondered what kind of lady would eventually catch your attention."

"Well, she caught my attention all right." If Mrs. Minnie only knew the whole story . . . she'd get a huge belly laugh out of it.

"Someone came into the restaurant the other day looking for somebody who fits her description."

Dillon's jaw hardened. Mrs. Minnie had to be talking about Constantine. His steps slowed. "Is that right?"

"The man looked awfully worried."

"What did you tell him?" Dillon asked.

Mrs. Minnie shrugged. "I told him I hadn't seen her. Because I hadn't."

That was a relief.

"What did this guy look like?" Dillon asked.

She shrugged again. "I don't know. He was handsome—in a big city kind of way. But there was something about his eyes . . . you could tell he was smart —but maybe not in a good way."

Dillon's back stiffened. "Did he say why he was looking for her?"

"Just that she was someone he cared about and that she was missing."

"Anything else about the man I should know?"

Mrs. Minnie shrugged. "I don't know. If I had to guess, he was in his forties maybe."

Forties? Constantine was in his early thirties, at the most.

Concern raced through Dillon. What if the man who'd come into Mrs. Minnie's wasn't Constantine?

What if they'd been looking for the wrong person this whole time?

CHAPTER FORTY-THREE

GRACIE WATCHED as Levi and Dani swayed to the music beneath the warm string lights. The way the newlyweds looked at each other caused something to crash in her heart.

They looked so happy, like they belonged together.

Belonging wasn't something she'd ever experience, was it? Not since her parents had passed. The whole balance of her future had been changed in a way she'd never imagined.

Her heart sagged at the thought.

"Hey," someone murmured beside her.

She looked up and saw Dillon standing there. He must have finished his dance with the woman who owned the restaurant. The two of them had looked like they were having such a good time out there on the dance floor.

If Gracie were honest with herself, she'd admit that the man looked entirely too handsome in his plaid shirt, jeans, and cowboy boots. Why did seeing him cause a round of tingles to go up her spine?

It made no sense.

Despite that, a smile fluttered across her face as she glanced up at him. "Hey."

His gaze followed hers as he leaned on the other side of the post. "Those two belong together, don't they?"

"I don't even know either of them, but it's clear there's something special between them." Before Gracie could stop it, a tear trickled down her cheek. She tried to wipe it away before Dillon saw it, but it was too late.

"Gracie?"

"I'm fine." She tried to wave him off.

Before she could convince him, he took her arm and led her outside. He kept walking until they reached a gazebo bordering the sound. The air felt crisp around them—not too hot but not too cold. The sky was clear with sparkling stars and a sliver of the moon. A slight wind swayed the sea oats near the shore, creating a soothing rustling sound.

Dillon's leg brushed hers as they sat beside each other on a wooden bench there. "What's going on?"

Gracie sucked in a deep breath, not even knowing where to start. She hadn't intended on sharing anything—just on coming and having a good time. But seeing this community . . . seeing the newlyweds . . . seeing Dillon dance with someone old enough to be his grandmother . . . it had stirred something inside her.

Maybe it had even broken something inside her.

"Gracie?" Dillon repeated.

The look in his eyes was that of warm concern and maybe even genuine care.

"It's just . . ." Gracie rubbed her lips together. "It's just that . . . you deserve to fall in love like Levi and Dani, Dillon. I took that chance away from you. You'll never have a reception like this where you dance with the love of your life in front of all the people who care about you."

"You took that chance away? Gracie, I'm a grown man. I make my own choices."

"I know you feel like that now." She sniffled and looked away, unable to gain control of her emotions. "But one day, you're going to get over Lauren. You're going to want more than what I can give you."

"I'm already over Lauren, Gracie. This isn't about her."

She looked back at Dillon again, still bewildered that her opinion of the man had changed so quickly. But she'd had him all wrong.

Dillon was a good man, and Gracie had put him in a bad situation, whether he acknowledged that or not.

"I feel like . . ." How did she say what she needed to say? Gracie paused before finally trying again, "I feel like I've brought tragedy into your life. It wasn't fair of me. It was selfish."

"What do you deserve, Gracie?" His voice was just above a whisper.

She shivered as she thought about his question. "I . . . I don't know, to be honest. I just want to make my parents proud."

"I'm sure they would be."

"I'm not so sure."

"Gracie . . ." Dillon said her name softly.

She waited, fully expecting him to agree that she was an absolute failure.

How could she make this right?

How could she undo the mess she'd made?

When Dillon didn't say anything for another moment, her gaze fluttered to his. The look in his eyes made her breath catch.

He didn't look angry or frustrated or even accusatory.

What was that emotion?

As if in slow motion, he leaned toward her and murmured, "You didn't ruin my life, Gracie. Please don't ever think that."

"But . . ." How did Gracie convince him that she had?

Before she could even start, Dillon reached for her. He brushed his fingertips across her jaw. Tugged her hair back from her face. Soaked in her gaze.

Gracie froze, hardly able to breathe.

Electricity danced on her skin. Through her blood. Made her bones ache.

His lips covered hers.

She halfway expected something passionate or demanding.

Instead, Dillon's lips felt tender against hers.

His hand went to her waist, and he nudged her closer. As he did, Gracie reached for him. Her hands rested on his chest, not to push him away.

Not even close.

Nothing else mattered at the moment. Only the scent of his woodsy cologne and shaving cream. The feel of his surprisingly soft lips. The hardness of his body as he gradually pulled her closer and closer.

Gracie knew that this moment was like a pendulum—swinging in the past to put all the other kisses she'd experienced to shame. Swinging in the future as a defining moment she'd never forget.

Because she'd never been kissed like this before.

Nor had Gracie ever felt so much warmth and electricity from a man she initially couldn't stand.

DILLON HADN'T PLANNED on kissing Gracie.

But he'd be lying if he said he regretted it.

No, kissing her had been one of his best decisions ever.

For now, he sensed that she needed space to process what had just happened.

He extended his hand to her as she sat quietly beside him, her eyes wide and her motions still.

"How about we get back to the reception?" he asked quietly.

"Great idea." Gracie stared at his hand for another second before smiling and slipping her fingers between his. Hand in hand, they walked back into the barn, where the party was still in full swing.

Dillon could see his future with Gracie.

Which was crazy.

She was from the city. Spoiled. High maintenance.

Except she wasn't.

His first impression of the woman had been wrong. Gracie didn't mind getting dirty or offering a helping hand. She'd even injured herself in order to save his life.

He'd been so wrong.

As soon as he figured out who was stalking her, maybe the two of them would actually have a chance together.

But who was this person? Dillon was beginning to doubt that Constantine was the only person at play here. Could someone else be behind the crimes? Or was Constantine simply working with another man?

Dillon had almost brought the subject up as he and Gracie were sitting in the gazebo. But another part of him didn't want to ruin the moment.

Couldn't they just have one moment together without talking about this? It only seemed fair. They'd have plenty of time to talk through these things later.

But for now, Dillon just wanted to enjoy the rest

of the reception and pretend like everything was okay.

"Would you like to dance?" He glanced at Gracie, waiting for her response.

"I would love to."

Still holding her hand, he led her to the dance floor and pulled her close. He felt her heart pounding against his chest. Smelled her flowery shampoo. Relished her soft skin.

Just as their dance started, the tune switched from a medium tempo number to "The Keeper of the Stars." The song was old, but it had always been one of Dillon's favorites.

He and Gracie swayed together there for a moment.

Dillon felt happier than he had in a long time. Happier than he ever thought he would feel again. God had known what He was doing when He created the woman in his arms.

As the song ended, Dillon stepped back and glanced at Gracie. He saw the same affection in her gaze that he felt for her in his heart.

Dillon opened his mouth, unsure what was about to come out of his lips.

But before any words emerged, he froze.

What was that smell?

He couldn't be sure, but it almost smelled like . . . smoke.

Was something on fire?

Alarm raced through him.

He had to find out.

CHAPTER FORTY-FOUR

GRACIE STEPPED BACK, getting out of Dillon's way as he and Colby rushed outside.

What was going on?

She sniffed.

Was that smoke? Was something on fire?

She glanced around, looking for the source, but she saw nothing.

Certainly, if this barn was on fire, they would have evacuated. Still, she felt uneasy as danger crackled through the air.

Again.

There seemed to be a lot of that lately.

The mystery smell was just a coincidence, Gracie assured herself.

Not some kind of distraction that Constantine had caused to get Dillon away from her.

Gracie shivered and rubbed her arms.

She hated living in this kind of fear. She missed the days when she didn't have to look over her shoulder. Would those times ever return?

Sometimes it felt like they never would.

Then she remembered her kiss with Dillon, and hope rushed through her veins. Maybe she *could* have a happy future. If that kiss was any indicator. . . then she definitely could.

Because she wanted to experience more of Dillon's lips against hers. The kiss had felt like more than a kiss . . . it seemed to be a promise of a beautiful beginning.

The truth was Gracie didn't even want to take over her parents' company. It wasn't in her wheelhouse. She could be perfectly content to stay on this island and make a life for herself here.

But she didn't want the wrong person to get their hands on White Star Media either.

Philip was the perfect person for the job.

Philip . . .

Gracie squeezed her eyes shut and prayed he was okay.

She'd checked a couple of times today to see if there were any updates.

No one had seen or heard from him.

As his image lingered in her mind, she heard someone behind her.

Before she could react, someone clutched her arm.

She gasped. Tried to turn. Tried to think.

Instead, someone pulled her into the darkness behind her.

A gloved hand covered her mouth as the shadows consumed her. The man's other arm stretched across her chest, rendering her immobile.

Constantine? Had he managed to sneak in and find her?

Panic surged through her.

But she couldn't scream.

Couldn't do anything.

She was at this man's mercy.

"Finally," a gruff voice whispered. "Some time alone with you."

DILLON RUSHED around the side of the barn and glanced in every direction.

Where was the smoke coming from?

He halfway expected to see a fire.

Instead, he spotted some hay smoldering by an outbuilding in the distance.

He motioned to Colby, and they sprinted toward the site.

Still no flames.

That was a good sign.

Using his foot, Dillon pushed some of the straw away.

Then he sucked in a breath.

A smoke bomb had been planted there.

"Why would someone leave that?" Colby stared at the firework and shook his head. "Just to be mischievous?"

Dillon's jaw hardened. He wished that was what had happened.

But he had a feeling there was more to it than that.

He had to get back inside.

He had to find Gracie.

Now.

CHAPTER FORTY-FIVE

"LISTEN CAREFULLY," the man growled into Gracie's ear. "Tonight at two a.m. you're going to go out the front door of your home, walk to the left, and stop at the intersection four houses down. I'll be waiting for you with further instructions."

Fear shot down her spine. Who was this man? Constantine?

She wasn't certain. His voice was too low, too muted.

"But—" she tried to say, despite the hand over her mouth.

The man loosened his grip just slightly.

"Shh. Don't talk. There will be all the time in the world for that later. You'll want to hear this next part. I have a bomb planted in your husband's bedroom.

If you as much as whisper to him what's going on, I'll make the whole house go—" He made an exploding sound.

Her blood froze.

Gracie had no doubt this man was telling the truth.

"What do you want from me?" Her voice quivered, and she dared not speak too loudly out of fear he would do something to harm these people she'd started to care about.

"You'll find out soon enough. As long as you cooperate, we won't have any problems. Understand?"

She remained silent.

"Understand?" he repeated, his hand wrapping around her neck until her airway clogged.

She nodded. "Yes. Yes! I understand."

"If I have to repeat myself, you won't like it. And if you speak a word of this to anyone . . . this whole place will go up in flames."

"What do you mean?"

"I mean, I had my guy wire the place."

She sucked in a breath. "No . . ."

"I did. He also set up cameras, so if you try to skirt around my rules . . . there will be consequences."

The freeze rushing through Gracie's veins dropped to subzero.

This man meant his words. She had no doubt about that.

Gracie was going to have to leave Cape Corral, wasn't she?

Just when things were falling in place.

Tears rushed to her eyes.

How was Dillon going to handle another woman walking out on him?

DILLON RUSHED INTO THE BARN, nearly running into Emmy.

He grasped her arms. "Have you seen Gracie?"

She shook her head, her eyes instantly widening with alarm. "No, I haven't. Is she okay?"

"I don't know." Dillon's gaze darted around. "But I need to find her."

"I'll help you look." Emmy took off through the barn, helping Dillon to search the faces in the crowd.

Had someone grabbed her? Had they used that smoke bomb as a ruse to lure Dillon away?

His gut clenched. He hoped he was overreacting.

But he didn't think he was.

Dillon pushed through the people milling around, desperate to put his eyes on Gracie. But a bad feeling brewed in his gut.

As he darted toward the back of the structure, he nearly collided with someone who stepped from a stall.

"Gracie?" He grasped her arms, almost unable to believe his eyes. He'd been so certain she was in danger.

She looked as startled as he felt as she stared up at him. "It's me. Is everything okay?"

Relief washed through him. "It is now. I thought . . ."

She swallowed hard enough that her throat visibly tightened.

"That something happened to me?" she finished.

"Yes, that something happened to you. I'm so glad it didn't." He folded her into his arms.

Her arms wrapped around him also, and she leaned into his embrace. She held on tighter than he expected, but Dillon didn't complain.

"I was just trying to get out of the way," she explained.

Dillon glanced behind her at the dark stall she'd stepped out of, surprised she'd want to disappear into such a place. But he still had so much to learn about the woman. He looked forward to every moment of it.

"I think we should get you back to the house," he finally murmured.

"I think that's a great idea."

Dillon slipped his arm around her and led her to his truck.

Thank God, Gracie was okay.

He wouldn't forgive himself if something happened to her.

CHAPTER FORTY-SIX

WHEN GRACIE and Dillon got back to the cottage, she turned to face him.

"It's been a really fun day, but my head is pounding," she said, regret churning inside her. "If it's okay, I'm going to turn in for the evening."

Dillon stared at her a moment, as if trying to read between the lines. Finally, he stepped back and nodded. "I understand. It has been a long day."

"Yes, it has." Gracie smiled up at him, unable to resist the motion.

Despite everything, Dillon had brought a new hope inside her. There was a lot to be said for that. No one in the sixteen years since her parents died had managed the task.

But Gracie desperately needed to be alone so she

could digest what had happened tonight. So she could let the tears flow. So she could face up to the future without trying to conceal her emotions.

Dillon took her hand, brought it to his lips, and gently pressed a kiss there.

Shivers went down Gracie's spine at the chivalry of it all. She may have just accidentally married her perfect man, only to have to walk away from him.

"We can talk more in the morning," he murmured.

Her heart leapt into her throat at the tender sound of his voice. "That sounds great."

But Gracie knew there would be no talking in the morning.

She would be long gone.

She swallowed a cry until she could make it to her room.

Dillon couldn't know what she was planning.

If he found out, the bomb would destroy his house.

Gracie couldn't take that chance.

GRACIE HAD to write her goodbye letter four times. Her tears kept smearing the ink—a dead giveaway that she didn't mean the words she scribbled.

Finally, she managed to produce a clean copy.

She glanced at the time on the alarm clock on her nightstand.

It was one thirty.

She needed to leave soon.

Walking down the road would only take a few minutes, but she had to figure out how to sneak out of the house without Dillon finding out. He was the type who heard every creak.

But if she wasn't successful, his life would be on the line.

She had to keep reminding herself of that fact because, in truth, all she wanted was to run into Dillon's arms and tell him everything. He had a way of making it seem like life would be okay, like he could handle whatever the world threw his way.

Gracie muffled another cry.

How had it come down to this?

Of course, Constantine was going to get his way.

Except . . . the man who'd pulled her into the shadows at the barn . . . he hadn't sounded like Constantine.

Then again, he could have been disguising his

voice.

But he hadn't smelled exactly like Constantine either.

Gracie shook her head.

Maybe her mind was playing tricks on her.

With one more glance at the room, she placed the letter on her neatly made bed.

There was no need to bring anything with her.

She'd come with nothing and would leave with nothing.

She twisted the doorknob, trying to be extra careful.

She stepped into the hallway and tiptoed down the hall.

No Dillon.

Gracie had done it.

She'd managed to make it this far without waking him.

She prayed that the person behind this didn't go back on his word and detonate that bomb anyway.

DILLON SAT up in bed with a start.

What was that sound?

He'd barely heard it. But, from somewhere in his

house, a squeak had cut into the silence.

Almost like his front door had opened.

His back muscles stiffened.

He threw the covers off and stood, pulling on some clothes.

Without wasting any time, he opened the door to the hallway and glanced around.

Nothing.

That didn't stop him from checking out the rest of the place.

He stepped out and surveyed everything around him again.

Everything appeared to be in place, best he could tell.

He paced down the hallway and into his living room.

Still clear.

His kitchen.

Also clear.

Nothing caught his eye.

Had he heard Gracie in her room? Was she okay?

Dillon hesitated a moment before walking to her door. He paused outside and drew in a deep breath.

He wasn't sure Gracie would welcome being awakened.

But he wouldn't be able to sleep until he knew

she was okay.

He tapped his knuckles on the wood.

There was no answer.

He tried again.

Still no answer.

The bad feeling in his gut churned harder.

"Gracie?" he called.

When silence echoed back, Dillon twisted the door handle.

Gracie's bed stared at him, neatly made and untouched.

Something had been left on top of the white bedspread.

Was that a letter?

Dillon's heart pounded in his ears as reality tried to settle in his mind.

It couldn't be . . . this wasn't . . .

But he knew it was.

With trepidation in his heart, Dillon sat on the edge of the bed, opened the crisply folded paper, and began reading.

He felt like he'd done this before.

Read a goodbye letter.

Probably because he had.

A SHARP WIND whipped around Gracie, and she pulled her sweater closer.

As she stepped out onto the sandy street in front of Dillon's house, she looked back at his cottage one more time.

In the short period since Gracie had been here, this place had begun to feel a lot like home. Against all the odds. Against her wishes. Against her expectations.

More tears pressed at her eyes.

Gracie had no idea what the next hour would hold. What the day would hold. What the rest of her life would look like.

But she was glad she'd had this time here on Cape Corral to help her find her balance and clear her head.

Now she had the biggest battle of her life to fight.

It would be so much easier if there wasn't so much at stake. This was about more than her life.

It was about Dillon's. About her parents' company. Maybe even about something much, much bigger than all that.

If there was one thing Dillon and the people in this town had taught her, it was to stand up for what she believed in. To fight. To not back down to bullies.

A sharp wind swept over the landscape, blowing Gracie's hair from her face.

She couldn't let people with nefarious intentions gain control of her parents' company. But she knew these people would stop at nothing to do so. They would threaten the people she cared about in order to persuade her.

Like they'd threatened Dillon now.

A knot formed in her throat.

Was there really a bomb in his house?

She didn't know, but she couldn't take any chances.

Please, Lord . . . protect him!

Gracie continued down the road, the sand padding her footsteps.

Everything around her was quiet and still on the island. The lights inside people's homes were out, and an inky darkness filled the air, making it nearly impossible to see.

As Gracie reached the corner where she was supposed to meet the man, she paused.

She'd only stopped for a minute when something came down over her head.

A hood.

Then a familiar voice said, "I knew you'd come."

CHAPTER FORTY-SEVEN

DILLON STARED at the words that had been written in a neat script on the notebook paper in his hands.

I'm sorry, Dillon, but I can't do this anymore. I was wrong to think our marriage would work. I know you took me into your home, and, for that, I'm grateful. But we can't live this make-believe life anymore.

I'm leaving.

I have a plan.

Don't come look for me.

You'll be okay. I promise.

I'll be okay also.

Time is ticking away, and we must be mindful of our next steps and not do anything rash.

Memories rushed back to Dillon.

Memories of Lauren.

Of the note she'd left him.

It had been eerily similar as she'd talked about how she couldn't do it anymore as a military wife.

Pain crashed in Dillon's heart.

How could Gracie have left like this? Especially after everything they'd overcome? They'd made so much progress—even just tonight.

Dillon should have known.

He should have never let his heart get involved.

He leaned back on the bed and shut his eyes.

His mind raced.

Where would Gracie go at this time of night? Had she gotten a ride with someone? With Uber Stan and Water Taxi Mel?

It was a possibility, he supposed.

Dillon looked at the note again.

Time is ticking away . . .

The wording seemed odd for Gracie.

His breath caught as another thought hit him.

What if . . . what if this note wasn't what it first appeared?

What if there was more to this story and if Gracie was trying to send him a subtle message?

Dillon jumped to his feet.

He didn't know if that was the case at all.

But Dillon needed to find Gracie.

He needed to catch her before she left this island.

If she was leaving, she needed to tell him face-to-face.

And if she'd left this note for other reasons . . . then it was even more important that Dillon find out the truth.

CHAPTER FORTY-EIGHT

GRACIE COULD HARDLY BREATHE.

It was partially the situation.

Partially the bag over her head.

Partially plain fear.

But she felt like she was going to suffocate.

"What are you going to do with me?" she asked, her voice more high-pitched than she'd like.

She'd been tossed into the backseat of a pickup, and the vehicle rumbled over the sand.

At least two people were with her right now.

Constantine and Uncle Max, she assumed.

They'd said very little.

"You'll find out," one of the men muttered.

Was that her uncle's voice? Was it Constantine? Why was Gracie questioning it now?

Who else would the voice belong to?

"You know the bridge leading to this island is closed," she muttered.

"Don't you worry your pretty little head over any of this," the man said. "We have a plan. If you hadn't messed it up in the first place, we wouldn't be here right now. We wouldn't have had to go to these extreme measures—and your life wouldn't be on the line."

Part of her wanted to cave. Wanted to tell them she would do whatever they wanted.

But she remembered Dillon and the saltwater cowboys here on Cape Corral. They fought for what they believed in. They sacrificed. They didn't give up.

Gracie needed to draw on some of that inspiration.

But she also had to be careful.

She was nowhere as strong as Dillon. It would be hard to defend herself physically.

Which meant she would need to use her other capabilities to do so.

As the truck pulled to a stop, her lungs tightened.

What were these men going to do now?

DILLON LEFT his truck at the stable. The vehicle was loud and couldn't get in between tight spaces.

He saddled Blaze then took off in a search throughout the island.

There was no way for anyone to leave this place quickly.

That could work in Dillon's favor right now.

He'd already called backup. Levi, Grant, Dash, and Colby knew what was going on and were on their way to help.

Even though Dillon figured Gracie was still on Cape Corral, that didn't make the situation any less urgent.

He had to find her—and the sooner, the better.

If Gracie had really left him because she couldn't live with their marriage, then he would deal with that.

But Dillon's gut told him there was more to the story.

He wouldn't rest easy until he found out the truth.

As Blaze galloped along, Dillon searched the dark spaces around him, looking for any signs of life. Most people here on the island were sleeping right now, which, in some ways, made this easier. He didn't have to search curious faces or answer any questions from citizens.

So where had Gracie gone?

How far could she have gotten? If Dillon's instinct was correct, she'd only left thirty minutes ago.

As his phone rang, he saw it was Levi.

"We figured out where Constantine was staying earlier," Levi said. "It was late, so I didn't tell you. Anyway, we came out here to his place."

Dillon's lungs froze as he anticipated a shift. "And?"

"He's here. And he's tied up."

"By whom?"

"He didn't see anyone's face. The person said he couldn't get in the way anymore, though. However, he claims he doesn't know where Gracie is."

But if not Constantine then . . . who?

Dillon remembered what Mrs. Minnie had said, how she'd indicated the man she'd seen was older than Constantine.

There was someone else at play here.

"Come on, Blaze." Dillon nudged his horse. "Faster. We can't let Gracie get away—not without talking to her first."

Blaze picked up his pace.

But Dillon had already searched this side of the island.

The only part that was left was up by the North Banks—Ferguson territory.

He knew where he had to head next.

CHAPTER FORTY-NINE

AS ROUGH HANDS jerked her from the truck, Gracie tried to identify the voices.

Who was Constantine working with? Uncle Max? His brother, Angelino?

She couldn't be sure. The hood over her head prevented her from seeing their faces.

Whoever it was, he pushed her across the sand so hard that it was sure to leave a bruise.

"Where are we going?" Gracie could only assume they were headed toward a boat off the island.

"You ask a lot of questions," the man muttered.

"I'm not going anywhere," she argued. "What would it hurt to tell me what's going on now? It's not like I can tell anyone."

"You want to know what's going on?" The man

stopped on the sand. "You're going to sign some official documents giving up control of White Star Media."

She'd figured that much. "Why all the theatrics? Why go through this much trouble?"

"Because nothing else we tried worked."

"Then why is this hood over my face? Why is everything cloaked with darkness right now?"

"You really want to see what's going on?"

"I do." But Gracie's voice trembled as she said the words.

"Fine." The man forced her to turn, manhandling her as he shoved her in the opposite direction.

Then he jerked the hood off.

In front of her was a helicopter.

That's how these guys planned on getting off the island.

But when Gracie looked behind her, she didn't see who she thought she would.

No, it wasn't Constantine or Uncle Max or even Angelino standing there leering at her.

"ANY LUCK FINDING HER?" Grant's voice rang through the phone.

"Not yet," Dillon said. "I'm headed toward the North Banks."

"You think that's where they are?"

"It's my best guess."

"Dash and Colby are in Wash Woods right now looking. I'll head your way to give you a hand."

"I appreciate it. Thanks."

As Dillon crossed to the other side of the dune, the mansions the Fergusons had built for themselves and their clan appeared.

Dillon paused for long enough to scan everything around him. In the distance, he saw the lone water tower that had been erected on this side of the island. It always seemed out of place among the houses. But, for now, it remained here.

Was someone from the Ferguson family working with someone who may have taken Gracie?

Dillon had no idea.

As he started forward, he heard something in the distance.

What was that?

Then he realized what it was.

That almost sounded like a . . . helicopter.

CHAPTER FIFTY

"PHILIP?" Gracie's mouth dropped open. "What . . . ?
Why . . . ?"

He shrugged, his scrawny body puffed up as if he
were a giant. A smug expression stretched through
his eyes, through the curl of his lips.

The look made nausea swirl in Gracie's stomach.
How could this slick businessman have turned into
this monster?

"I've worked my entire life to build this company
to be what it is." His nostrils flared. "I can't hand over
the reins to someone who has no idea what she's
doing."

"But Philip . . . my parents trusted you."

"At the time, they should have. I would have
done anything for them. But sixteen years have

passed, Gracie. I've built this company into what it is today, and I'm not going to let someone else take that from me."

"But Constantine . . ." She struggled, trying to make sense of everything.

Philip shrugged. "He and I go way back. Really, most people have a price. You just have to name it, and they'll do whatever you want to do. Same for your uncle Max. I'm sorry that he had to get involved with this, but neither of us think that you're the person who should take over."

Her hands fisted at her sides. "But this company belonged to my parents. They believed in me. It's rightfully mine."

"You don't even understand what kind of weight and power running this company holds," Philip continued. "We're on the cutting edge of the news world. Our editorials have changed the way people think. I'd even like to say that they've changed how our country is shaped. I can't just let anyone have that power."

"Your job isn't to have that power anyway," Gracie said. "Your job is to be objective and to present the facts."

He shrugged as if the idea was unfathomable.

"All I need you to do is to sign those papers. I

already have them all drawn up. I'll take you up to my office in DC, and we'll get it done."

"And then?" Gracie almost didn't want to hear his answer.

"And then . . ." He shrugged again. "Then you'll be useless to us. I'm afraid you're going to be in a tragic accident."

Her blood went even colder. "Philip, you don't want to do this."

"Believe me, I do. I've been thinking about it for a long time. If you had just married Constantine, I wouldn't have had to go through all this. I wouldn't have had to get involved like this."

"I'm surprised you got your hands dirty. You were always the kind to let other people do the dirty work."

"I could only risk a couple of people knowing what's going on. I'm smart enough to know that. Now, come on. Let's go."

He took her arm and shoved her toward the helicopter in the distance.

Gracie knew that as soon as she got inside, that there would be no going back.

She glanced back at the town of Cape Corral.

Soon this would be a distant memory.

Gracie held back a cry at the thought of it.

DILLON REACHED the area just as the helicopter began to lift into the air.

No!

How was he going to stop them from getting away?

He only had one idea.

And it wasn't a great idea.

But he was out of other options right now.

He pulled the rope from his saddle and made a lasso. Maybe all those contests he and his friends had shared together might pay off.

As he formed the knot, Grant rode up beside him. "What in tarnation do you think you're doing?"

Dillon began to swing the rope in the air as he nodded at the helicopter. "I'm going to try to lasso them."

Grant's eyebrows shot up in the air. "You really think that's going to work?"

"I saw it on a YouTube video once. Some guy from Brazil did it." Dillon shrugged. "I don't know what else to do."

"At least it's a small helicopter, one of the lightweight ones. Maybe you stand a chance. Maybe."

Dillon continued to circle the rope before launching it into the air.

But it missed the landing skid of the helicopter probably by two feet.

He frowned.

But he wasn't giving up.

He just had to act more quickly. Before they got too high.

He circled the rope in the air again before launching it again.

This time, it caught the landing skid.

Dillon jerked the rope, tightening the knot there.

But he needed something besides himself and Grant to secure this rope. If Dillon held on, he'd soon be flying through the air like a kite.

He needed to think of something else.

Now.

CHAPTER FIFTY-ONE

"WHAT IS HE DOING?" Philip grumbled beside Gracie, holding a gun in his hand.

She glanced out the window, and her heart leapt into her throat.

Was that . . . Dillon and Grant?

It was dark outside and hard to make out details.

But it almost looked like they were trying to . . . lasso the helicopter.

Would that even work?

She had no idea. But, despite that, she found herself smiling.

Dillon had come for her.

Now she just needed to pray that his plan would work.

She continued to stare out the window, wondering exactly how this would play out.

Moments later, she felt a tug.

Had Dillon done it? Had he actually lassoed the helicopter?

Hope surged inside her.

She felt another tug just then.

That definitely seemed to be what happened.

"Russo, what's going on?" Philip yelled. "We need to get out of here."

"I know, Boss. But something is wrong."

Gracie fought a smile.

Dillon had come to the rescue. Just like always.

But she knew that this was a long way from being over.

"WE NEED to get to the water tower," Dillon said.

Grant nodded beside him. "Let's do it."

Still holding on to the rope, Dillon and Blaze galloped to the metal structure. He had to wrap this rope around it. It was the only thing nearby that was strong enough to keep this helicopter from flying away.

Even if they managed to get this rope tied, Dillon

didn't know what that might mean would happen next.

But he would figure that out when the time came.

He felt the rope tug harder in his hands and knew he didn't have much time.

Soon he would literally be at the end of his rope. And he'd be forced to make a decision about whether he needed to hold on and be carried away or release the rope and let go of Gracie forever.

Moving quickly, he wrapped the rope around one of the legs of the water tower. Grant rode up alongside him just in time to help pull the knot tighter.

Then they backed up.

It looked like they'd done it. They'd effectively tied the helicopter in place.

But that still didn't mean that Gracie was safe.

She was still up there with someone.

Not Constantine.

But someone equally as dangerous.

CHAPTER FIFTY-TWO

"PULL UP ON THE THROTTLE! Try harder!" Philip yelled.

"There's no use," Russo said. "We can't go anywhere."

"There's got to be something we can do!"

"I need to land this before I burn up the clutch. Then we'll all be goners."

"There's no way we're landing. If you even try to, I'll shoot you." Philip raised his gun toward the man.

Gracie held her breath.

Philip was serious. He'd pull that trigger if it came down to it.

Gracie had no idea what that would mean for everyone on board.

But it wouldn't be good.

The helicopter seemed to groan as it pulled against the rope.

Gracie glanced out the window.

Dillon and Grant stood below, watching everything as it happened.

She couldn't just sit here helplessly.

She had to do something.

Making a split-second decision, she gripped the side of the door and swung her feet out.

"Stupid girl! What are you doing?" Philip tried to grab at her.

Before he could, Gracie released her grip and grabbed the landing skid.

She hung there a moment. Her arm ached.

Had she split her cut open and pulled out the stitches?

It didn't matter. Not right now. Not when her life was on the line.

The helicopter seemed to waver in the air.

As it did, her grip loosened a moment.

But she held on.

Now she just needed to get to that rope.

And then she could get down to safety . . . to Dillon.

"WHAT IS SHE DOING?" Grant muttered.

Dillon's muscles tensed as he watched the scene play out. "She's trying to get away."

"Jumping Jehoshaphat . . . she's going to kill herself."

"Maybe not. She's a pretty determined lady."

"What if her grip slips?"

Dillon couldn't get that question out of his mind either.

He climbed back on Blaze. "I'm going to get closer. Just in case she needs me."

"We have more trouble," Grant said.

Dillon glanced up and saw a man leaning from the helicopter.

Was that Philip? The CEO of White Star Media?

It was dark, but that's who it looked like.

And the man had a gun in his hands.

A gun that was aimed at Gracie.

Dillon clucked his tongue, and Blaze took off toward where Gracie was dangling on the rope.

A gunshot filled the air.

Gracie screamed but held on.

Philip had missed, it appeared.

But Dillon didn't like where this was going.

He nudged Blaze faster.

Another gunshot split the air.

That's when Dillon realized that this guy wasn't aiming for Gracie.

He was aiming for the rope she was holding on to, trying to split it so he could still get away.

Dillon's gut clenched as he realized the implications of it.

If that rope split, Gracie was going to go hurtling toward the ground.

To her death.

He and Blaze trotted closer and closer. As they did, Gracie continued to climb down the rope, dangling with the wind. Every time the breeze kicked up, he sensed her fear. Concern ricocheted through him.

He looked back, only for a minute. Near the water tower, Grant had his gun aimed at Philip.

Everything seemed to happen at once.

Philip fired again.

The rope split.

Grant fired at Philip, causing the helicopter to begin spinning in circles.

CHAPTER FIFTY-THREE

GRACIE FELT HERSELF FALLING.

Saw the helicopter circling.

Heard the gunfire.

She squeezed her eyes shut.

Dear Lord . . . help us now! Please!

It was at least a twenty-foot fall to the sandy ground below.

Her body wouldn't survive that.

Especially not if the helicopter crashed on top of her.

She braced herself for the pain that was sure to come.

Until she felt something swoop beneath her.

She sucked in air, hardly able to breathe.

Was this what death felt like? Smooth, hard, and fast?

"I've got you, darling."

She plucked her eyes open.

Dillon . . .

Dillon had caught her.

While riding Blaze.

She blinked, trying to make sure she wasn't dreaming.

Based on the way Blaze galloped, causing her body to bounce, she wasn't.

Before she could ponder it too long, she heard a crash behind her.

Gracie looked over her shoulder and saw that the helicopter had gone down.

Flames erupted near the engine.

Was Philip dead? Russo?

Dillon pulled up on the reins, and the horse stopped. They turned to look at the carnage of the accident.

As they did, Philip and Russo crawled from the door, trying to get away.

Levi and Dash pulled onto the scene just as Grant rushed toward the men, ready to make an arrest.

Maybe the worst of this was over.

Maybe.

DILLON NEVER WANTED to let Gracie go.

As he climbed off Blaze, Gracie slid off and into his arms. She nearly fell into his embrace.

At the moment, nothing else mattered.

Nothing except holding her.

"You came for me . . ." she murmured.

"What kind of husband would I be if I didn't?" Dillon tried to keep his voice light, despite the fact he clutched Gracie against his chest.

He'd come so close to losing her.

He never wanted that to happen again.

She pulled back—just slightly—and he saw the tears glistening in her eyes. "Thank you."

"Why'd you leave like that? You could have told me."

"He said he'd planted bombs at your house . . . at the barn . . . and listening devices." She shook her head. "I couldn't take any chances. He might have been bluffing, but I don't think he was."

"Oh, Gracie . . ."

"You could have been killed . . ." she murmured.

"So could you." Dillon nudged her back, just enough that he could see her face.

Gracie was so beautiful—on the inside and the out.

Dillon had been so wrong about her.

He leaned down until his lips met hers.

Gracie reached up, and her arms wrapped around his neck as she pulled him closer.

Everything else around them disappeared.

For a moment, it was just him and Gracie . . . and whatever their future looked like.

CHAPTER FIFTY-FOUR

"OF COURSE, I knew something was up with the two of you," Marla said. "This is a small town. People talk. The fact that Dillon McGrath had married someone he'd known less than twelve hours was big news."

Gracie squeezed Dillon's hand as they all rode together to a community Thanksgiving celebration.

"I'm sorry we didn't tell you," Dillon said.

Marla waved her hand in the air. "Oh, it's okay. It's just good to see you happy. Sometimes, you don't need to know each other a long time. When it's right, it's right. Other times, love can bloom when you least expect it."

Yes, love could bloom when you least expected it. Gracie liked that analogy.

The past three weeks had been a whirlwind.

Gracie had been able to look Constantine in the eye and tell him exactly what she thought of him. Apparently, her ex-fiancé had tried to back out of his agreement with Philip. Philip hadn't liked that, so he'd tied Constantine up and promised to come back for him later.

That hadn't happened. Levi had found Constantine first.

Meanwhile, both the barn and Dillon's house had been searched. There were no explosives or listening devices inside either. Philip had just been blowing smoke in order to manipulate Gracie, and it had worked.

Dillon had gone with Gracie up to DC to handle business matters with White Star. With Philip in jail—along with Constantine and Max—Evan, the company's senior vice president, was now in charge.

And Gracie really liked him.

A week after that, Gracie had a birthday.

She'd officially become the primary stakeholder of the company. She'd attend board meetings and have some say in what happened. But she wouldn't run the day-to-day operations.

Instead, she'd found an online program that

would allow her to go back to school to get her law degree.

She would make her parents proud by becoming the best businesswoman she knew to be.

And Dillon had been by her side and supportive of her every decision.

She squeezed his hand again.

He'd been a true blessing to her—as had their marriage.

They pulled up to Smith's Hope and parked. There had to be at least thirty cars already outside.

Dillon had said this would be a night to remember, and Gracie already couldn't wait.

They climbed out and headed toward the doors together. Gracie was surprised they were closed, but she supposed that was to keep the heat in.

As Dillon pulled them open, joyous rounds of "Surprise!" flew from inside.

Gracie's hand flew over her heart when she saw everyone staring at them.

Then her gaze went to the banner that had been strung in the distance, which read, "Congratulations Dillon and Gracie."

"What?" she whispered.

Dillon grinned at her. "Surprise!"

Emmy and Colby stepped from the crowd.

"We never got to celebrate your marriage as a town," Emmy explained. "And we wanted to do something to show you both that we're here for you."

Gracie's hand went over her mouth. She didn't even know what to say.

"I thought . . . I thought this was a Thanksgiving dinner," she finally murmured.

"It is," Dillon told her, pointing to a long table stretched across the middle of the barn. "But it's also a reception."

He stepped back and showed her the dance floor that had been set up on the other end of the barn, complete with those string lights, hay bales, and a band playing in the corner.

As "The Keeper of the Stars" began floating through the air, Dillon took her hand. "May I have this dance, Mrs. Gracie McGrath?"

She grinned. "Yes, you may."

Dillon led her onto the floor before wrapping his arms around her waist. Gracie rested her head on his chest as they swayed back and forth.

"You knew about this?" she asked.

"I did."

"It's . . . it's really nice, Dillon."

"I didn't want you to miss out."

"How'd you even know I would like something like this?"

"I saw the way your eyes lit up when you watched Levi and Dani dancing."

She let out a rumbling chuckle. "Underneath all this bravado, you do have a sensitive side."

"Shh. Don't tell anyone."

She giggled again. "I'm really happy, Dillon."

"I am too."

She pulled her head back so she could look him in the eyes. "I love you. Now and forever. And my love for you is just going to keep growing."

His lips curled in a smile. "I love you too, Gracie McGrath."

~~~

Thank you so much for reading *Cape Corral Keeper*! Dillon and Gracie's story really came alive in my mind, and I had a great time writing this book.

If you enjoyed *Cape Corral Keeper*, I'd love for you to leave a review and/or tell a friend about it! Reviews truly do help authors get more visibility.

Stay tuned for *Seagrass Secrets*!

COMPLETE BOOK LIST

Squeaky Clean Mysteries:

#13 Cold Case: Clean Getaway

#14 Cold Case: Clean Sweep

#15 Cold Case: Clean Break

#16 Cleans to an End (coming soon)

While You Were Sweeping, A Riley Thomas Spinoff

The Sierra Files:

#1 Pounced

#2 Hunted

#3 Pranced

#4 Rattled

The Gabby St. Claire Diaries (a Tween Mystery series):

The Curtain Call Caper

The Disappearing Dog Dilemma

The Bungled Bike Burglaries

The Worst Detective Ever

#1 Ready to Fumble

#2 Reign of Error

#3 Safety in Blunders

#4 Join the Flub

#5 Blooper Freak

#6 Flaw Abiding Citizen

#7 Gaffe Out Loud

#8 Joke and Dagger

#9 Wreck the Halls

#10 Glitch and Famous (coming soon)

Raven Remington

Relentless 1

Relentless 2 (coming soon)

Holly Anna Paladin Mysteries:

#1 Random Acts of Murder

#2 Random Acts of Deceit

#2.5 Random Acts of Scrooge

#3 Random Acts of Malice

#4 Random Acts of Greed

#5 Random Acts of Fraud

#6 Random Acts of Outrage

#7 Random Acts of Iniquity

Lantern Beach Mysteries

#1 Hidden Currents

#2 Flood Watch

#3 Storm Surge

#4 Dangerous Waters

#5 Perilous Riptide

#6 Deadly Undertow

Lantern Beach Romantic Suspense

Tides of Deception

Shadow of Intrigue

Storm of Doubt

Winds of Danger

Rains of Remorse

Torrents of Fear

Lantern Beach P.D.

On the Lookout

Attempt to Locate

First Degree Murder

Dead on Arrival

Plan of Action

Lantern Beach Escape

Afterglow (a novelette)

Lantern Beach Blackout

Dark Water

Safe Harbor

Ripple Effect

Rising Tide

Crime á la Mode

Deadman's Float

Milkshake Up

Bomb Pop Threat

Banana Split Personalities

The Sidekick's Survival Guide

The Art of Eavesdropping

The Perks of Meddling

The Exercise of Interfering

The Practice of Prying

The Skill of Snooping

The Craft of Being Covert

Saltwater Cowboys

Saltwater Cowboy

Breakwater Protector

Cape Corral Keeper

Carolina Moon Series

Home Before Dark

Gone By Dark

Wait Until Dark

Light the Dark

Taken By Dark

Suburban Sleuth Mysteries:

Death of the Couch Potato's Wife

Fog Lake Suspense:

    Edge of Peril

    Margin of Error

    Brink of Danger

    Line of Duty

Cape Thomas Series:

    Dubiosity

    Disillusioned

    Distorted

Standalone Romantic Mystery:

    The Good Girl

Suspense:

    Imperfect

    The Wrecking

Sweet Christmas Novella:

    Home to Chestnut Grove

Standalone Romantic-Suspense:

    Keeping Guard

    The Last Target

    Race Against Time

    Ricochet

Key Witness

Lifeline

High-Stakes Holiday Reunion

Desperate Measures

Hidden Agenda

Mountain Hideaway

Dark Harbor

Shadow of Suspicion

The Baby Assignment

The Cradle Conspiracy

Trained to Defend

Mountain Survival (coming soon)

Nonfiction:

Characters in the Kitchen

Changed: True Stories of Finding God through Christian Music (out of print)

The Novel in Me: The Beginner's Guide to Writing and Publishing a Novel (out of print)

ABOUT THE AUTHOR

USA Today has called Christy Barritt's books "scary, funny, passionate, and quirky."

Christy writes both mystery and romantic suspense novels that are clean with underlying messages of faith. Her books have won the Daphne du Maurier Award for Excellence in Suspense and Mystery, have been twice nominated for the Romantic Times Reviewers' Choice Award, and have finaled for both a Carol Award and Foreword Magazine's Book of the Year.

She is married to her Prince Charming, a man who thinks she's hilarious—but only when she's not trying to be. Christy is a self-proclaimed klutz, an avid music lover who's known for spontaneously bursting into song, and a road trip aficionado.

When she's not working or spending time with her family, she enjoys singing, playing the guitar, and exploring small, unsuspecting towns where people have no idea how accident-prone she is.

Find Christy online at:
www.christybarritt.com
www.facebook.com/christybarritt
www.twitter.com/cbarritt

Sign up for Christy's newsletter to get information on all of her latest releases here: www.christybarritt.com/newsletter-sign-up/

If you enjoyed this book, please consider leaving a review.

Made in the USA
Middletown, DE
23 May 2024

54752158R00220